Suddenly David saw it.
Something unbelievable
was moving through the sky.

Whoa! David thought. His jaw dropped open, and his eyes widened with wonder.

It was a round form that looked almost like a baseball rolling in slow motion. It seemed to be traveling at about the height at which an airplane flew. Though there was a haziness about the form, David couldn't tell if it was made of a gas or solid substance. Strangest of all, the form had a bright green glow.

David realized his heartbeat had doubled in speed. He wasn't sure if he was experiencing excitement or fear—or both. He told himself to calm down so he could better study the phenomenon. When he heard Joe come out of the house, David pointed upward and said, "Look!"

"Wow!" Joe exclaimed. "What is it?"

"I wish I knew," David replied.

wishbone™ *Mysteries*
titles in Large-Print Editions:

CASE OF THE ON-LINE ALIEN

by Alexander Steele

WISHBONE™ created by Rick Duffield

Gareth Stevens Publishing
MILWAUKEE

This book is a work of fiction. The characters, incidents, and dialogues are products of the author's imagination and are not to be construed as real. Any resemblance to actual events or persons, living or dead, is entirely coincidental.

For a free color catalog describing Gareth Stevens' list of high-quality books and multimedia programs, call 1-800-542-2595 (USA) or 1-800-461-9120 (Canada). Gareth Stevens Publishing's Fax: (414) 225-0377.

Library of Congress Cataloging-in-Publication Data

Steele, Alexander.
    Case of the on-line alien / by Alexander Steele; [interior illustrations by Genevieve Meek].
      p. cm.
    Previously published: Allen, Texas; Big Red Chair Books, © 1998.
    (The Wishbone mysteries; #9)
    Summary: After witnessing an eerie glow in the sky, Wishbone begins to worry about aliens landing on Earth, especially when he hears a strange humming sound in the neighborhood.
    ISBN 0-8368-2449-0 (lib. bdg.)
    [1. Dogs—Fiction. 2. Mystery and detective stories.] I. Meek, Genevieve, ill. II. Title. III. Series: Wishbone mysteries; #9.
    PZ7.S81446Cas   1999
    [Fic]—dc21   99-18949

This edition first published in 1999 by
Gareth Stevens Publishing
1555 North RiverCenter Drive, Suite 201
Milwaukee, Wisconsin 53212 USA

© 1998 Big Feats! Entertainment. First published by Big Red Chair Books™, a Division of Lyrick Publishing™, 300 E. Bethany Drive, Allen, Texas 75002.

Edited by Kevin Ryan
Copy edited by Jonathon Brodman
Cover concept and design by Lyle Miller
Interior illustrations by Genevieve Meek
Wishbone photograph by Carol Kaelson

Printed in the United States of America

1 2 3 4 5 6 7 8 9 03 02 01 00 99

To Corrine, for her love, support, and dog knowledge

FROM THE BIG RED CHAIR . . .

Oh . . . hi! Wishbone here. You caught me right in the middle of some of my favorite things—books. Let me welcome you to the WISHBONE MYSTERIES. In each story, I help my human friends solve a puzzling mystery. In *CASE OF THE ON-LINE ALIEN*, the citizens of Oakdale witness an eerie green glow in the sky— many suspect a UFO. It is up to David and me to discover the source of this . . . uh . . . mysterious occurrence.

The story takes place in the spring, during the same time period as the events you'll see in the second season of my WISHBONE television show. In this story, Joe is fourteen, and he and his friends are in the eighth grade. Like me, they are always ready for adventure . . . and a good mystery.

You're in for a real treat, so pull up a chair and a snack and sink your teeth into *CASE OF THE ON-LINE ALIEN*!

Chapter One

Wishbone tilted his head in confusion. He watched a patch of white fog drift over the next-door neighbor's yard. Fog wasn't so unusual, but this particular fog was floating low enough for the dog to jump up and touch it.

I'd better check this out, the white-with-brown-and-black spots Jack Russell terrier thought. *I like to know exactly what's going on in my neighborhood. Especially at night.*

Wishbone crept carefully into the neighboring yard, passing an opened garage door on the way. He approached the fog, its whiteness all the more eerie against the darkened sky.

Suddenly a thought drifted into Wishbone's mind. *Wait a second. That's not fog. It's a cloud. And I know exactly where it's coming from. David's science project!*

Wishbone spun around and trotted toward the garage he had just passed. A visit to this particular garage was always fun for Wishbone, because in addition to being a regular garage, it was also a laboratory.

Wishbone entered the garage, his nails clicking on the concrete floor. Along the right wall stood metal shelves filled with a variety of tools, gadgets, equipment,

7

and supplies. In front of the shelves an interesting invention was on display. It consisted of a glass tank about the size of a bathtub. The tank stood on four shiny steel legs, and it was filled with water. Underneath the tank lay three propane burners, all of them now hissing as they released a bluish flame.

In front of the invention stood a boy, rubbing his lower lip with his fingers, deep in thought. This was David Barnes, a fourteen-year-old whom Wishbone knew extremely well. David had curly black hair and large, dark eyes that never stopped observing the world with curiosity. He was an absolute whiz at doing anything electrical, mechanical, or generally scientific. On top of that, he was a really nice guy who sometimes slipped Wishbone a treat.

"Hi, David," Wishbone greeted.

David didn't seem to hear, but Wishbone figured that was because he was concentrating. David picked up a small container and sprinkled a powdery substance into the water. Then he picked up another container and sprinkled in a different powdery substance. Next, he picked up a long wooden spoon and stirred the water as if he were preparing a mystical witch's brew.

"Hellooo!" Wishbone said, scratching at the floor to make his presence known. "It's Wishbone, paying a visit to your top-secret laboratory. Sorry, but I forgot my security pass."

Without taking his eyes off his invention, David said, "Hi, there, Wishbone. Welcome aboard, boy. I'm just making some adjustments on my project."

Wishbone knew about David's science project. It had recently won first place in the regional finals of the Young Scientist Competition. Now the project was on its way to the national finals, which Wishbone figured was something like the World Series of science projects.

David crouched down and turned knobs on each of the three propane burners. All three of the bluish flames rose a few inches higher. "Bet you're wondering what this is all about," David said as he stood.

"On the contrary," Wishbone informed David, "I know exactly what this is all about. It's a proposed solution for dealing with the 'greenhouse effect.' You heat up the water, pour in that powdery stuff, and—*presto!*—instant cloud. You're suggesting that this type of cloud could be made on a grand scale to screen out some of the sun's harmful radiation. This'll buy us time until we can figure out how to fix that messy carbon dioxide problem. Or . . . something like that."

David kept his eyes focused on the tank of water.

He isn't even listening to me, Wishbone thought with a sigh. *People don't think I understand science simply because I'm a dog. Imagine that!*

Vapor drifted upward from the water and, several feet above the tank, began forming into another cloud.

David said to himself, "Good, it's thicker this time."

Wishbone sat down and gave his side a good scratch with his back paw. "The whole thing is really very impressive, David. You know, when you're done with this, I've got an idea for another project—a machine that automatically opens the refrigerator when a dog barks. But, of course, your project is also of value."

Catching a familiar scent, Wishbone turned his head. Like most dogs, Wishbone prided himself on having a highly refined sense of smell. As the brand-new cloud drifted *out* of the garage, Joe Talbot stepped *into* the garage.

"Hey, David," Joe remarked, "I see you've got your head in the clouds again."

"Very funny," David said, his eyes following the cloud's floating course.

Joe was David's friend and next-door neighbor. He had straight brown hair and a great smile. Sports were Joe's main thing, especially basketball. Wishbone lived with this good-natured guy and considered the boy his very best friend in the world.

"How's the project going?" Joe asked.

"Pretty well," David replied. "I'm just doing a little fine-tuning in preparation for the national finals."

"Well, if you feel like taking a break," Joe said, "how about you and I going to Pepper Pete's? It's Friday night. Sam will be there."

Wishbone's ears perked up. There were few places as exciting to him as Pepper Pete's. It was a restaurant that served pizza, pizza, and more pizza.

David wiped his hands on his pants. "I guess I've done enough brain work for the night. Pizza sounds like a great idea."

"Correction," Wishbone said. "It sounds like a *brilliant* idea!"

"I just need to clean up in here and leave my parents a note," David told Joe. He spent a few minutes shutting down his cloud-making machine and putting things away. Then he disappeared through the door leading into the house, and returned a minute later. After leading Joe and Wishbone out of the garage, David pushed a button on a small device he carried and, with a whir, the garage door closed automatically.

Everything is operated by remote control these days, Wishbone thought. *Except refrigerators.*

"Now I need to leave my mom a note," Joe said as Wishbone and the two boys walked to the Talbots' house. Wishbone knew that David's parents, little sister, and Joe's mom had all gone to see a movie together.

Joe ran inside his house, and David waited by the

10

porch. Wishbone lay in the cool grass of the yard. It was a beautiful spring night. Wishbone's nose took in the pleasant scents of new buds on the shrubs. He also caught a whiff of Mexican food coming from the Hernandez house down the block.

Wishbone looked up at the night sky. It looked like a big black blanket speckled with tiny diamonds. He picked out the brightest star, which also happened to be his personal favorite—Sirius, otherwise known as the Dog Star.

Then Wishbone's eyes detected something unusual up there. The dog sprang to his feet and focused his vision. At first he thought he might be seeing another one of David's clouds, but then he realized it was something much weirder.

David looked up to see what had caught Wishbone's attention. The night was very clear, the stars sharply defined. David always found the night sky to be a beautiful sight. He picked out the constellations of Orion and the Big Dipper, and then the planet Mars, which he knew had a faintly reddish tint.

Suddenly David saw it. His jaw dropped open, and his eyes widened with wonder. Something unbelievable was moving through the sky.

Whoa! David thought.

It was a round form that looked almost like a baseball rolling in slow motion. It seemed to be traveling at about the height at which an airplane flew. Though there was a haziness about the form, David couldn't tell if it was made of a gas or solid substance. Strangest of all, the form had a bright green glow.

11

David realized his heartbeat had doubled in speed. He wasn't sure if he was experiencing excitement or fear, or both. He told himself to calm down so he could better study the phenomenon. When he heard Joe come out of the house, David pointed upward and said, "Look!"

"Wow!" Joe exclaimed. "What is it?"

"I wish I knew," David replied.

"I'll go get Miss Gilmore," Joe said, leaping off the porch. "I'm sure she won't want to miss this."

Joe dashed toward Wanda Gilmore's house, which was next door to Joe's house, on the side opposite David's house. David kept his eyes locked on the glowing object. Even though it appeared to be moving slowly across the sky, David knew it was probably traveling quite fast. As he squinted, David noticed the green form glowed more brightly toward its center. The color, the brightness, the motion—everything about this sight was at the awesome level.

David heard Joe knocking and calling out, "Miss Gilmore, come take a look at this thing in the sky!"

Wanda Gilmore opened her front door and said, "What sort of thing in the sky?"

"I think it's a UFO!" Joe said excitedly.

David turned to see Wanda charging out of her house like a race car on the last lap of a championship race. Unfortunately, she was wearing fuzzy pink slippers instead of rubber tires. One of the slippers slipped, causing Wanda to sway wildly to and fro before she regained her balance.

"Oh, my gosh," Wanda said when she finally looked up at the green glow. "Oh, my *gosh!*"

Wanda was a wonderfully unusual person with an offbeat taste in clothing. At the moment, she was wearing paisley patterned pants with a matching headband.

David knew Wanda would be especially interested in the green glow, because she had had a lifelong fascination with things like ghosts and UFOs.

Wanda and Joe moved to the Talbots' yard, both of them keeping their faces angled to the sky. The green glow continued its rolling horizontal path, but David noticed it was now dimming. It seemed to be evaporating like steam being absorbed into the air. After several more seconds, the glowing green form had completely vanished.

"It's gone," Joe whispered.

Once more the sky appeared as normal as it did any other night. David was glad the other two people were present. Otherwise, he might have been tempted to believe the whole episode had been a trick played on him by his imagination.

Everyone stood for a moment in silence. Wanda spoke first. "I don't know about you guys, but I think it might have been . . . well . . . something from another planet!"

Wishbone jerked his head toward Wanda, as if alarmed by that comment.

Joe knelt down to give his dog a reassuring scratch on his back. "Miss Gilmore, you may be right," Joe said. "That thing sure didn't look like anything natural. And it sure didn't look like anything made by man. So what does that leave us with?"

Although David was no less impressed by the green glow than Joe and Wanda had been, he wasn't one for jumping to conclusions. "I hate to disappoint you," he said, "but I seriously doubt that was an alien spaceship."

Wanda rubbed her lower back as if it were bothering her. "How can you be so sure? Unidentified flying objects are spotted all the time—all over the world. And, sure, a lot of them are spotted by unreliable witnesses. But, then, a lot of them are spotted by very responsible people. Like us. And since a lot of those unidentified flying objects are never identified, doesn't it make sense that some of them *could* be alien spacecrafts? Don't you think that it's at least a possibility?"

Over the years, David had done quite a bit of research on UFOs and aliens. And, like most kids his age, he had seen numerous movies, television shows, and comic books that dealt with those topics. Though David found all of this stuff fun and interesting, he had come to the conclusion that none of it was real.

"To this day," David told the others, "there is not one piece of hard scientific evidence proving that an alien spacecraft has ever visited the planet Earth. Besides, from a scientific viewpoint, it would be almost impossible for it to do so."

"Then what do you think that thing in the sky might have been?" Wanda asked.

"There are all kinds of natural events that cause weird sights in the sky," David explained. "Meteors, comets, and a few other phenomena. I'm almost positive that thing we saw was just a fantastic show put on by Mother Nature."

"You may be right," Wanda admitted. "However, it didn't look natural to *me*."

"Me, either," Joe added.

Wanda looked at her watch. "Oh, you know what? I'd better drive over to the newspaper office and make sure we get a report on this thing for tomorrow's edition. It's already eight o'clock. We don't have a lot of time." Wanda owned the town's newspaper, *The Oakdale Chronicle*, which she had inherited years ago from her father.

"If it's okay," Joe told Wanda, "David and I will ride over with you. We were just on our way to Pepper Pete's."

15

"Great," Wanda said, as she hurried toward her house in her fuzzy slippers. "Just let me slip on some proper footwear."

Joe continued to scratch his dog's back. "What did you think of that thing, Wishbone? It was awfully strange, wasn't it?" Wishbone almost seemed to give a nod.

David's eyes swept over the black sky and glimmering stars. Ever since he had been a small boy, David had been curious about what things were and how they worked. He remembered his amazement the first time he really noticed the television set and the telephone, and the cars that zoomed by. He had pestered his parents until they gave a satisfactory explanation for each of those things. Though David didn't say it, it bothered him quite a bit now that he couldn't make an accurate identification of the mysterious green glow.

"Yes," David said to himself quietly. "That thing was awfully strange."

Chapter Two

"Hey, there, strangers!" Samantha Kepler said with a warm smile, as David, Joe, and Wishbone entered Pepper Pete's. Sam was carrying a tray with a steaming-hot pizza sitting on it. David saw Wishbone immediately glue his eyes to the food.

"Hi, Sam," David and Joe said at the same time.

Sam was an outgoing girl with silky blond hair and hazel eyes. She was highly creative and always willing to lend a helping hand to someone in need. Sam went to school with David and Joe, and the three of them were so close that David thought of them as a team.

"Did you guys see that glow in the sky?" Sam asked.

"You bet we saw it," Joe answered. "We were standing in my front yard, and suddenly—there it was!"

As Sam shifted the pizza tray to her other hand, David saw Wishbone follow its path very carefully. Sam had begun to work part-time at Pepper Pete's back when her dad bought the restaurant, and she had become a major help to him.

"Some guy came running in here and said there was a UFO overhead," Sam told her friends. "So practically everyone in the restaurant went racing out to have a look. I want to talk to you guys about this some more, but first I'd better get this pizza to its destination."

As Sam carried the pizza toward a table, David, Joe, and Wishbone made their way through the restaurant. David always enjoyed going to Pepper Pete's. As it usually was on a Friday night, the place was crowded and loud with conversation. Oakdale was a small town, and there weren't a lot of other places to go for entertainment at night. The decor featured brick walls, red-and-white-checked tablecloths, and a rocking jukebox. The place was so casual, Sam's father didn't even mind that Wishbone came there on a regular basis.

As Joe and Wishbone headed for a vacant table, David stopped at a table occupied by two boys he knew from the school Science Club. Though the two boys were friends, they made an odd pair. Toby O'Shaughnessy was probably the shyest kid David knew, and Gilbert Pickering was probably the most confident.

"Evening, gents," Gilbert said. He had swept-back blond hair and wore a pair of round glasses. Gilbert dressed on the preppie side, and a lot of the kids found him too stuck-up for their liking. David, however, was able to appreciate the boy's sharp intelligence.

David gave a wave. "Hi, Gilbert, Toby."

Toby muttered something.

"Excuse me?" David said, not quite hearing.

"I said, 'Good to see you.'" Toby spoke louder. Toby often spoke so low that understanding him was no small challenge. He was a very nice kid, but his red hair and clothing always looked as if they had just been through a tornado.

"Did you guys catch a look at the green glow?" David asked.

18

Toby nodded, and Gilbert said, "We saw it on the way over here. Toby and I both think it was some kind of natural phenomenon."

"I agree," David said.

"Then we're in good company," Gilbert commented. "After all, this is coming from the man chosen to compete in the national finals of the Young Scientist Competition."

Mention of the contest caused a look of discomfort on Toby's face. To cover it up, he reached for a slice of pizza, but somehow he managed to send his soft drink sliding across the table. Gilbert stopped the glass just before it fell over the edge.

"Thanks," Toby said, a bit embarrassed.

Realizing the contest might be a sore subject, David shifted to another topic. "You know, Gilbert, maybe you should feature the green glow on your next program."

Even though Gilbert was only fourteen, he had his own talk show on the local radio station, WOAK. It was a half-hour weekly program called *Youth Viewpoint*.

Gilbert took off his glasses and gestured with them. "Exactly my plan. As soon as I got here, I went straight for the pay phone and called my uncle. He's an aeronautical engineer. He does a lot of cutting-edge research, and I figured he could shed some light on whether or not the phenomenon might have been a flying vehicle. But, unfortunately, he won't be able to come to town for my next show."

Toby muttered something.

"Excuse me?" Gilbert asked.

"I said, 'Too bad,'" Toby repeated.

"Anyway," Gilbert continued, "now I need to come up with another guest or two. If you guys get any ideas, let me know. I need to line someone up as soon as possible."

"Will do," David said. Then he headed toward the back of the restaurant, where he joined Joe at a table.

David saw Wishbone sitting on the floor, wagging his tail with pleasure.

Soon Sam came by, setting two glasses of soft drinks on the table, and a small bowl of water on the floor. "I brought everybody his regular to drink. Now, what can I get you fellows to eat?"

"Does a medium pizza with pepperoni sound okay?" Joe asked David. David gave a thumbs-up.

Sam glanced down at Wishbone and said, "Is that all right with you, boy?"

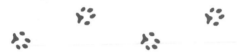

"Pepperoni will do just fine," Wishbone told Sam. "And I don't mean to rush you, Sam, but I haven't eaten a thing in at least two hours. Thanks."

Sam gave Wishbone a wink, then walked away from the table.

David picked up a packet of sugar and fiddled with it. "I'm not real comfortable talking about my science project with those guys."

"Why not?" Joe said after a sip of his soft drink.

Wishbone looked up from his water bowl. "Yeah, why not?"

"Both Toby and Gilbert entered the Young Scientist Competition, but neither of them made it to the regionals," David explained. "And they both had great projects. Toby's dealt with atomic structure, and Gilbert's dealt with the way dolphins use ultrasonic frequency to detect objects underwater. But, as luck would have it, I'm the one who made it to the regionals, and now I'm on my way to the nationals."

Joe nodded. "And you think they might be jealous of you?"

"Maybe not Gilbert so much," David said. "He likes the spotlight, all right, but he's got the radio show and all sorts of other things going on. But I think Toby really had his hopes up about going the distance with his project."

"He'll be okay," Joe said.

"Sure, he'll bounce right back," Wishbone said from his spot on the floor. "Speaking of bouncing, Joe, have you seen that little red rubber ball of mine? I was playing with it yesterday in the living room, and now I can't seem to find it anywhere."

Before Wishbone got an answer, he turned to see the door of the restaurant swing open. Damont Jones swaggered in as if he owned the place. Damont played with Joe on the school basketball team. The boy had recently gotten a buzz cut to make himself appear tougher, and there always seemed to be a mischievous look on his face.

"I see a table in back," Damont said to an older boy who followed him inside. Wishbone recognized the other boy as Damont's nineteen-year-old cousin, Brewster Kidd. Brewster's long brown hair was pulled back in a ponytail, and he wore a black T-shirt displaying the words "We will find the truth!" Brewster was bigger and huskier than Damont, but he, too, showed the mischievous look. Wishbone figured this was a family trait.

Damont and Brewster made their way to the table right next to Wishbone. The two cousins sat down. Brewster turned his baseball cap around backward, and Damont, who was also wearing a cap, did the same.

"Check out Damont," Wishbone told his companions. "He thinks he's cool because he's hanging out with a college kid."

David and Joe exchanged waves with Damont and Brewster, then continued their conversation. A few minutes later, though, when the song on the jukebox ended, Brewster stood up.

"Ladies and gentlemen," he called out loud enough for everyone in the restaurant to hear, "may I have your attention?"

"What's he doing?" Wishbone asked Joe and David. "I don't remember anyone hiring him to be the evening's entertainment."

Conversations in the restaurant faded to a low level. Brewster cleared his throat and spoke. "As some of you may know, my name is Brewster Kidd. I am a sophomore at Oakdale College. I'm also involved in the international search to uncover the truth about UFOs."

The restaurant grew even more quiet. Wishbone could tell that people were interested in UFOs that night.

"As you may be aware," Brewster continued, "there was unusual activity in the skies over Oakdale a short while ago. I believe there's a strong possibility that this green glow came from an alien spacecraft."

A low murmur moved through the restaurant.

"I know many of you saw the green glow," Brewster pressed on. "And I'd be grateful if you could assist me in reporting the event. If you *did* witness this activity, I urge you to check in at my Web site. There you'll have the chance to record your deceptions . . . uh, I mean perceptions . . . of what you saw. I'll forward these to the proper authorities, and they'll be a great help for confirming what happened."

Damont stood up and announced, "Here is the Web site address: 'WWW dot Brewster's UFO Quest.'"

"'Dot com,'" Brewster whispered to Damont.

"'Dot com,'" Damont added.

"Say the whole thing," Brewster whispered.

"Here it is again," Damont announced. "The address is: 'WWW dot Brewster's UFO Quest dot com.'"

Wishbone looked up at David and Joe. "What are these guys? The local alien-busters?"

"If you didn't get that address, or if you're not on-line," Brewster told the crowd, "please feel free to stop by my table. Thank you very much for your cooperation."

"You're so welcome," Wishbone responded.

The announcement done, Brewster and Damont sat down in their seats. The conversation in the restaurant continued, though not as loudly as before. Some of the customers looked amused, others confused, and a few actually went over to speak with Brewster.

Joe and David leaned in toward each other so they could talk without being overheard. Wishbone raised his ears to pick up the conversation.

"I've met that Brewster before," Joe told David. "But I never knew he was so into UFOs."

"Me, either," David said. "Personally, I'm not crazy about these UFO nuts. They get people all stirred up over nothing. Case in point."

David nodded his head in the direction of the neighboring table. Wishbone turned to look. Brewster was now talking with two teenage girls who seemed to hang on his every word.

"Do you really think that might have been a flying saucer?" one of the girls asked with awe.

"I think it was some type of alien vehicle," Brewster answered.

"Not necessarily a saucer," Damont said, leaning back in his chair. "More like a . . . well . . . just an alien vehicle."

"Get a load of Damont," Wishbone remarked. "Now he's trying to impress the *señoritas*."

"This is so cool," the other teenage girl said with a giggle. "And do you think aliens have come to Earth before?"

Brewster gave a firm nod. "There is no doubt that extraterrestrial creatures have visited this planet many times."

David couldn't resist turning around and throwing in his two cents. "Brewster, that's not really true. In fact, there's not a single piece of real evidence that supports your statement."

Brewster craned around to face David. He practically shouted, "False, false, false!"

Several customers at nearby tables turned to see what the noise was about. David looked uncertain about whether he wanted to continue the conversation. But now there was an audience waiting for his response.

"Listen," David said calmly, "scientists are fairly certain there is no intelligent life anywhere near our solar system. So if there is intelligent life in the universe, it's bound to live, say, a hundred light-years away. Now, even if those aliens have the fastest craft possible, do you know how long it would take them to reach Earth?"

Wishbone gave his right side a scratch. "Uh . . . just give me a second to figure this out."

David continued. "It would take them a hundred years. Because a light-year is the distance an object can travel moving at the speed of a light for a full year. And it is impossible for anything to travel faster than the speed of light."

"Says you," Brewster argued.

"Says the laws of physics," David stated. "As a moving object nears the speed of light, its mass increases so greatly that it would take an impossible amount of energy to make it go faster. A guy named Einstein proved that.

You may have heard of him. In other words, you can't just go zipping all over the universe the way they do in science-fiction movies."

Brewster got up from his chair and walked over to David's table. Wishbone could see this discussion was turning into a full-scale argument.

"That is a totally short-sighted view," Brewster declared. "Some people believe there *are* ways to beat the speed of light. What about hyperspace and wormholes?"

"Nice ideas," David said. "But unproven ones."

"Look," Brewster said, "we're talking about beings with an intelligence advanced beyond anything we can imagine. Who knows what they're capable of? It would be like comparing human intelligence to, say, that of canine intelligence." Brewster gestured at Wishbone.

"Hey, watch it!" Wishbone said in a growling voice. "I'm very intelligent. Quiz me on any subject—science, politics, cat-chasing."

"No matter how intelligent they are," David countered, "there's no way—"

Brewster cut him off. "Listen, man, you don't know what you're talking—"

At this point, Gilbert appeared. "Gentlemen, please," he said, holding up a hand, as if calling for a delay in battle. "I have a proposition for the two of you."

"Who are you?" Brewster asked.

"My name, sir, is Gilbert Stuart Pickering."

Brewster scratched his ear. "Oh, you're the kid who has that radio show. I've heard it once or twice. Not bad."

"Now you can do more than just listen to it," Gilbert said. "Sunday evening, *Youth Viewpoint* will be focusing on the UFO phenomenon, and the unknown glow that was seen tonight. I would like both of you to appear as guests on the program."

Wishbone rose to his hind legs. "Hey, what about me? All I have to do is bone up on the subject a bit and I'd be a terrific guest!"

"It should make for an exciting debate," Gilbert continued. "Both of you seem to know the subject well, and you have different opinions. Besides, I need to book someone right away."

"Sure, count me in," Brewster said.

David thought a moment, then said, "Okay, me, too."

"Excellent," Gilbert said. "The program will be broadcast live this coming Sunday at seven in the evening. Arrive at the WOAK studio at six-thirty so we can go over some details."

Brewster and Damont were both beaming as if they had just won the lottery. "You know what's really cool about being on the radio?" Brewster said to his cousin. "Radio waves break through the Earth's atmosphere and travel through space. Infinitely. In other words, it's possible that extraterrestrial beings will actually be listening to my voice!"

"That's a scary thought," Wishbone commented.

"Awesome," Damont said, giving Brewster a high-five.

"Is that true?" Joe asked David.

"Yes," David replied. "But those radio waves are also limited to the speed of light. So those aliens might not hear Sunday's show for a very long time."

Sam came over and threw an arm around David. "Way to go, David. One day you'll be famous throughout the universe!"

Chapter Three

"I hope I'll do okay on this radio show," David said, as he walked with Gilbert, Joe, and Wishbone along a quiet residential street. It was an hour later, and the group was headed homeward.

"Oh, you'll be great," Gilbert said, clapping David on the shoulder. "I guarantee it."

"You announce all the basketball games at school," Joe told David. "And everyone thinks you're terrific at that job."

"Here's the difference," David said. "When I announce the games at school, I'm just reporting what I see. But for this radio show, I'll have to be . . . well, just David Barnes. You see, I have a much better chance to make a total fool of myself."

The three boys chuckled at this remark.

"Nobody makes a fool of himself on my show," Gilbert said. "Well, that's not entirely true. There was a little trouble with one guest. It was an eight-year-old girl who was a highly skilled violinist. As soon as the show started, she . . . Oh, let's just say she forgot everything she ever knew, including her own name."

"Oh, thanks," David said jokingly. "That gives me a lot of confidence."

"Don't worry," Joe assured his friend. "I'll make sure you know your name that day. We'll practice it over and over."

"You know, it's really impressive what you do," David told Gilbert. "I mean, every week you go on the radio and talk to hundreds of people, most of them complete strangers."

"That's the way I am," Gilbert said with a touch of arrogance. "Gilbert Stuart Pickering always goes for the big challenge. But really, David, you have nothing to fear."

The group turned onto another block, where the night seemed even darker. The only illumination came from the occasional dim glow of a porch light. David saw Wishbone take the lead, as if to scout ahead for trouble.

"Speaking of aliens," Joe said, "have either of you read the book *The War of the Worlds?* I've got a copy at home, and I've been meaning to read it."

Wishbone turned his head, as if the book's title had somehow sparked his interest.

"Really?" David said, also with interest. "I've always wanted to read that book. And since it's about aliens, this might be the perfect time."

"I'll lend it you," Joe offered.

The boys walked in silence a few moments. Then David noticed a pleased expression on Gilbert's face. "What are you so happy about?" David asked.

"I was just thinking of *The War of the Worlds,*" Gilbert replied. "It's one of my favorites. And you know what? That was the very first story to deal with an alien invasion of Earth."

"Who wrote it?" David asked.

"Mr. H. G. Wells," Gilbert said. "For my money, the greatest science-fiction writer of them all."

"What else did he write?" Joe asked.

"He wrote *The Time Machine,*" Gilbert said, "which is about a mad scientist who travels thousands of years into the future. And he wrote *The Invisible Man,* which is about a mad scientist who discovers a formula that turns him completely invisible. And then there's *The Island of Dr. Moreau,* which is about a mad scientist who creates this breed of creatures that are half-man and half-beast. But I think *The War of the Worlds* is the most frightening of his books—even though it doesn't have a mad scientist in it."

"This guy sounds like my type of author," David said with a laugh.

Soon the boys and Wishbone reached the block where David and Joe lived. "Well, gents, and dog,"

Gilbert said, "it's time I bid you *adieu*. And, David, I'll see you Sunday night."

"I guess you will," David said.

"See ya," Joe told Gilbert.

As Gilbert continued on his way home, David, Joe, and Wishbone walked the last leg toward their houses. When they got to Joe's house, Joe ran inside, then returned a few minutes later with his copy of *The War of the Worlds*. Joe handed the book to David.

"Let me know how you like it. But no giving away the ending."

"Me? Never!" David said with a smile. "And thanks for the loan."

After entering his own house, David had a brief conversation with his parents, then went to his room. The walls featured posters of rock stars and scientists. The door contained a remote-control locking device that proved useful when David heard his little sister and some of her nosy friends approaching. At the moment, the floor was scattered with dirty clothes, but David figured he could pick them up tomorrow before his mom had to remind him.

David kicked off his shoes and climbed on his bed. He examined the hardcover copy of *The War of the Worlds*. It looked to be several decades old. The faded and slightly torn paper cover showed a color illustration of what seemed like a gigantic robot that was standing on three long legs.

David turned to the title page and noticed the book had first been published about one hundred years ago. He wondered if the story might seem somewhat out of date. But when David turned to Chapter One and began reading, he was pulled in by the book's very first sentence:

No one would have believed in the last years of the nineteenth century that this world was being watched keenly and closely by intelligences greater than man's and yet as mortal as his own.

Each page drew David deeper into the story. He read about how highly intelligent creatures on Mars were studying Earth because their own planet was cooling to a dangerous temperature. The Martians began drawing up plans for an attack on Earth. By the end of the first chapter, they launched a series of tube-like vehicles toward Earth and its unsuspecting people. David realized it might be an hour or two before he would be going to sleep.

Wishbone lay curled into his favorite sleeping spot, right at the foot of Joe's bed. The only sound in the darkened room was the slow and even breathing of both boy and dog. Wishbone was dreaming that he had dug a deep hole in the ground that led to a fancy restaurant catering only to dogs. A waiter hurried his way with a sizzling sirloin steak on a big platter. As he slept, Wishbone licked his chops.

Suddenly, Wishbone's ears stood up straight. Then he lifted his head. A noise had awakened him. The dog had especially sensitive hearing, which even allowed him to hear sounds that were too low or too high for humans to notice.

That's not a familiar noise, Wishbone thought. *It's not the refrigerator opening, or a clock ticking, or someone walking down the hall. It's . . . a very low humming sound.*

Wishbone raised his ears a bit higher. He determined

the sound was coming through the opened window right next to the bed.

It's probably just a mechanical gadget on the blink, Wishbone thought. *All the same, I'm the neighborhood chief of security, and whenever I sense something out of the ordinary, it's my duty to investigate.*

As quietly as possible, Wishbone jumped to the floor. He padded his way out of the room, down the staircase, across the living room, into the kitchen, and out the doggie door created especially for his own personal use.

The night's warm air washed over Wishbone's fur as he walked to the front yard. He stood still and listened very carefully. He heard a faint rustling in the trees, the constant chirping of a cricket, the flutter of several moths—and the low humming sound, which was now a few degrees louder.

What is *that sound?* Wishbone wondered.

The next second, Wishbone's fur bristled. He sensed that someone—or something—was watching him.

He turned his head slowly. Through the leaves of a shrub, he saw a pair of eyes glowing with a greenish-yellow luster.

At first he feared the eyes might belong to some dog-eating monster. But then his nose told him the eyes were only those of a common house cat. A hostile feline hiss confirmed the suspicion. Wishbone answered with a short growl, and the cat darted off into the night.

Cats, Wishbone thought. *Yeccch!*

Wishbone took a slow walk around the house, poking his black nose here and there. But the humming sound was so low, Wishbone was not able to determine where it was coming from.

He sat down and gave his side a thoughtful scratch. *Well, I still don't know what this humming is about. But*

33

there's no sign of a robber or a monster or an invading army of Martians. I guess I can say I've performed my duty for the night with honor. Now I can head back to Dreamworld.

Within minutes, Wishbone was back at the foot of Joe's bed, dreaming he was just about to sink his teeth into a gigantic steak. The meat was charred lightly on the outside, but tender and pink in the center. Just the way he liked it.

For now, he had forgotten all about the mysterious humming that was still outside the window.

Chapter Four

The next morning, Wishbone lay in a patch of sunlight that streamed inside through the kitchen window. He had already gobbled up his breakfast of kibble, which reminded him of steak for some reason, and lapped up a bowl of refreshing water. Now he was waiting for Joe to finish his breakfast so the two of them could get down to some serious play.

"Don't forget it's Saturday," Wishbone called up to the table at Joe. "And you know what that means. Time to play with the dog all day long!"

Joe didn't say anything. He was reading the newspaper as he ate from his bowl of cereal and milk.

I'll never understand why humans eat so slowly, Wishbone thought. *I think it's the main difference between people and dogs.*

Wishbone heard Joe's mother, Ellen, typing at the computer in the study. She was a librarian at the local library, and an amateur writer. Ellen knew more about books than anyone Wishbone knew—with the possible exception of himself. Wishbone thought about scampering into the study to see if Ellen was up for some play. But then he remembered she was working on a short story she wanted to finish writing over the weekend.

Wishbone gave a bark at Joe, in the hope that might hurry things along.

Joe looked at Wishbone. "Hold your horses. I'm reading about the green glow in the paper. It's very interesting. A reporter for the paper interviewed a professor of physics and astronomy from Oakdale College. And *she* doesn't even know what the green glow was!"

"Hmm . . . that *is* interesting," Wishbone said. "But we've still got a lot of playing to do. And, by the way, if you're not going to finish all your cereal—"

"You've already had your breakfast," Joe said, seeing the dog's eyes go to the bowl. "If you're getting restless, why don't you go outside and run around awhile? I'll be out there in a few minutes."

"Excellent plan," Wishbone said eagerly. "I'll see you outside. Don't be late!"

Wishbone darted through his private doggie door— and found himself in the middle of a glorious April day. The sky was a beautiful blue, and the birds were chirping like there was no tomorrow. The sun felt pleasingly warm, but not the least bit hot.

Okay, I've got a few minutes to kill, Wishbone thought. *What shall I do? I need an activity I can really sink my teeth into. I know—I'll dig up a bone!*

Wishbone made a beeline for Wanda's front yard. Scattered throughout the yard were small gardens of fresh dirt where Wishbone kept his personal supply of buried bones. It was irritating that Wanda kept the gardens overflowing with flowers, but Wishbone had learned to work around them as best he could. Wishbone selected a spot and prepared to dig. But then he stopped.

You know, he thought, *Wanda gets awfully touchy*

about my digging in these gardens. Maybe I should make sure she's busy before I get to work.

Wishbone trotted over to Wanda's house, the outside of which was a lot more decorated than the average home in Oakdale. It reminded Wishbone of the gingerbread house in *Hansel and Gretel*, only it wasn't made of gingerbread—or anything else edible. Wishbone climbed on top of a bag of fertilizer that leaned against the house and looked through a lacy curtain.

There was so much neat stuff in the living room, at first Wishbone didn't see Wanda. But then he noticed she was sitting in a chair reading the newspaper. And he noticed something else. As she sat there reading, Wanda was vibrating. Ever so slightly, her entire body was *vibrating.* She looked like a battery-operated doll whose batteries were low on power.

That Wanda is a funny one, Wishbone thought as he jumped down from the fertilizer bag. *But, no doubt about it, she's got the best dirt in Oakdale.*

Wishbone trotted back to his digging site and once

again prepared to dig. Then his ears picked up on something. It was the very same humming sound that had awakened him the night before. Wishbone realized it had probably been sounding all this time and he just hadn't noticed it—even though it was a bit louder by Wanda's house.

Ever since that green thing showed up in the sky, Wishbone told himself, *weird things have been happening all over the place. Now, where was I? Oh, yeah—bone!*

One more time, Wishbone prepared to dig. But before he could set his paws in motion, Joe stepped outside.

"Wishbone," Joe called. "Let's go see what David is up to."

Wishbone looked down at the dirt and said, "I'll see *you* later." Then he ran toward his best buddy, Joe.

When Wishbone and Joe reached the front yard of the Barneses' house, Joe headed for the door. But Wishbone didn't follow. Something had caught his eye. In the middle of the Barneses' front yard, some kind of object was glinting in the sunlight.

As Joe knocked at the door, Wishbone trotted over to the object, which was in the grass. It was a flat, rectangular thing about the size of a small pad of paper. The surface gleamed with a silver tone. Wishbone touched it carefully with his paw. It didn't feel like anything he was familiar with. He lowered his muzzle and took a good sniff. It didn't smell like anything he was familiar with, either.

Wishbone noticed one more thing about the object. A bizarre symbol was engraved on top of it. The symbol was definitely not familiar—a circle with a little squiggly figure in the center.

Here we go again, Wishbone thought. *Another weird thing in the neighborhood. I'd better take it to David. Maybe it fell off one of his inventions.*

Wishbone picked up the object in his mouth and carried it to the front door. Just then, David opened the door and said, "Hey, guys, how's it going?"

"Excushe me," Wishbone told David, still holding the silver object in his mouth. "Doesh dish bewong to you?"

David and Joe turned to look at Wishbone. "Hey, what's that you've got there?" David said to the dog.

"Beatsh me," Wishbone replied.

David took the object from Wishbone's mouth and examined it carefully. David ran a finger over the silver-toned surface. Then he pulled down the ends of the object, discovering it was somewhat bendable.

"What is it?" Joe asked.

David wrinkled his forehead. "I have no idea. I can't even tell what it's made from. It looks like metal. But it feels like ceramic tile. And it bends like rubber. This is very strange."

"Look," Joe said, pointing at the object. "There's a symbol engraved on it. Do you recognize that?"

"No," David said. "I wonder where Wishbone found this."

"In your front yard," Wishbone answered.

"I don't know," Joe said. "But it must have been close by. He didn't have time to go very far."

"I said I found it in David's front yard," Wishbone repeated. "Why is it no one *ever* listens to the dog?"

"Maybe it fell off a car or something," David said. "I'll give it a closer look later. Come on in."

David led Joe and Wishbone down the hall and upstairs into his room. Right away, Wishbone saw that the computer on the desk was lit up, and the screen was filled with information. Wishbone knew David was top dog when it came to computer know-how.

"What are you doing on the computer?" Joe asked.

David took a seat in his swivel chair by the desk. "I was checking out some Web sites that post UFO information. The Internet is crawling with them. Some of them are okay, but most of them are sort of silly."

Joe pulled up a chair beside David and sat down. Wishbone scratched his front paws against Joe's legs. "Hey, don't forget me. I like to surf the net, too, you know."

Joe lifted Wishbone onto his lap. "Have you taken a look at Brewster Kidd's Web site yet?" Joe asked.

"No, but that's a good idea," David told Joe. "Let's see . . . What was that address?"

"How could you forget?" Joe said humorously. "'WWW dot Brewster's UFO Quest dot com.' And don't forget that 'dot com'!"

As David typed keys, the two boys chuckled. Wishbone rested his paws on the desk, giving himself a front-row view of the computer screen.

"Ah, yes," Wishbone remarked. "Now all I need is a big box of popcorn."

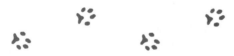

The screen turned midnight blue. Eerie synthesizer music played on the two plastic speakers. A silvery flying saucer appeared, whirling in mid-flight. David watched it lower slowly. When it landed at the bottom of the screen, the words "Brewster's UFO Quest" appeared above the image.

"Pretty nice graphics," David observed. "Now, let's see what he has to—"

A musical chime sounded, a sign someone was breaking in for an on-line conversation. David was used to this. Several of his friends were in the habit of breaking in to "chat" when they were on-line at the same time he was. Two people could do this with each other as long as they used the same on-line service.

"I wonder who's coming on," Joe said.

"We'll know in a second," David replied.

Suddenly the synthesizer music stopped, and the screen went pitch-black. The word "Hello" appeared in the middle of the screen. The letters glowed a fluorescent green. David was puzzled. He had never seen a message presented like that before.

"That's not how messages usually look, is it?" Joe asked.

"No, it's not," David said. "Normally these conversations take place in a little box at the top of the screen. And there's a screen name right next to the message. And normally the whole thing is in black and white. This is very weird."

"Can you send a response?" Joe asked.

David rubbed his chin. "I don't know. Usually there's a space under the dialogue box. I type my message there and then hit a button marked 'Respond.' But there's no place to do that now. Here . . . let me try something."

David typed the words: "Who are you?"

As he typed, the sentence appeared on the screen underneath the "Hello." Against the black background, the new letters glowed a fluorescent shade of purple. On a guess, David hit the "Return" key. Immediately, the purple words changed to green.

"Cool," Joe remarked.

"I think the change of color might mean that the message was sent," David said.

A fluorescent green symbol appeared on the screen, right underneath David's message. It was the exact same symbol as the one engraved on the object Wishbone had

found—a perfect circle surrounding a squiggly figure. David grew very curious to know with whom he was communicating.

"Aha!" Joe said, leaning forward. "The plot thickens. Whoever is sending these messages must have also left that silver object, with the same symbol, in your yard . . . or wherever it is Wishbone found it."

Wishbone looked at Joe as if he were upset by something he had just said.

David typed the words: "What does that symbol represent?" Again the words appeared in purple. Then, when David hit the "Return" key, they changed to green. The messages from before scrolled upward to make way for the new messages.

This message came back in green: "That symbol is the word for what I am. It is the name for my species. On your planet, you are known as a human. On my planet, I am known by that symbol."

"Oh, so you come from another planet," David spoke at the screen. "Yeah, right. I bet you do."

David knew someone was pulling his leg, but he

couldn't figure out who it was. He and his friends often had funny conversations on-line, but they seldom pulled pranks on one another. All the same, David decided to play along.

David typed and sent the following message: "What is the name of your planet?"

A message came back. "I could tell you the answer, but it would be another unfamiliar symbol. Humans have no name for my planet, but it is in the star galaxy humans refer to as the Milky Way. It is approximately nineteen light-years away from Earth."

"Wow!" Joe said in a low voice.

David saw Joe staring at the screen, awestruck, as if he believed the information coming through. David noticed that Wishbone was also watching the screen closely.

"You're not falling for this, are you?" David asked Joe.

"Uh . . . no," Joe said. "I guess not. Well . . . maybe."

David decided he would deal with Joe in a minute. He sent the following message: "Are you on Earth now?"

This message returned: "Yes. I arrived last night."

David sent: "Were you traveling in a craft that caused a green glow to appear in the sky?"

This returned: "Yes."

"This is major weird," Joe muttered.

David looked at Joe, then sent: "Are you communicating with other people on Earth, or just me?"

This returned: "Only you. I have been watching you since my arrival last night."

David wasn't sure why, but these words made him uncomfortable.

David sent: "Why have you been watching me?"

This returned: "I cannot reveal that information at this time. But we will communicate again. Soon. Good-bye."

All the green letters on the screen faded.

Chapter Five

Wishbone watched as the pitch-blackness of the screen gave way to the silver flying saucer. He was back at Brewster's Web site. The dog felt one of his ears flop down. He was a little stunned by what he had just viewed.

David turned to Joe. "Look, that wasn't really an extraterrestrial being. There's no way, okay? Somebody was playing a joke on me."

"Are you sure it was a joke?" Joe asked.

"Of course I'm sure," David replied. "Aren't you sure?"

"I'm not so sure," Wishbone said from his perch on Joe's lap. "Then again, I'm not sure that was a real alien, either. At this point, I'm not sure what I'm sure of!"

Joe ran a hand through his hair. "If it was just a matter of the computer conversation, I'd say that was definitely a joke. But there was that strange glow in the sky that no one can explain. And then there's this weird object that you can't identify. Okay, sure, it's a long shot, but you can't deny there's at least a one-in-a-thousand chance that might have been a genuine extraterrestrial!"

Wishbone smelled something in the air—the fascinating scent of a mystery. Immediately, his tail began to wag. He enjoyed a mystery almost as much as he enjoyed great books, delicious meals, and, well, life itself. Plus, with his high intelligence and superior senses, Wishbone knew he was especially skilled at detective work.

David was rubbing his lower lip with his fingers, thinking. "You're right, Joe. Sure as I am about this, I should always remain open-minded. All right, we'll investigate. But we'll do it the scientific way."

"What do you mean?" Joe asked.

"A person like Brewster jumps to conclusions," David explained. "These people assume something is true, and then they look for things that confirm their idea. But a true scientist works the opposite way."

"Like how?" Joe said.

"We'll start with a theory," David said, holding up a finger. "Namely, that I was just contacted by an E.T. Then we'll do everything in our power to prove that theory is *false*. If we fail to prove the E.T. was fake, then we'll begin to explore the possibility that it might be real."

"Great!" Joe said with excitement. "So how do we start this scientific investigation?"

"With the best source of information available," David said. "Let's see . . . Hey, why don't we pay a visit to that professor of physics and astronomy who was in the paper this morning? Dr. Marilyn Isaacs, I think her name was. It's Saturday, but she might be around the college campus. We can head over there right now."

"Uh . . . big as this thing is," Joe said with a sheepish look, "I'm afraid you'll have to go without me. I promised my mom I'd help her set up some things at the library. They're having a big fund-raising event tonight. But I was planning to meet Sam at her house around one. Maybe you could hook up with us there and give us a report."

David tapped a key, shutting down his computer. "Sure. I'll see you then."

Wishbone turned to Joe. "And I'll see you then, too, Joe. You don't think I'm going to miss a second of the mystery-solving, do you?"

David watched Dr. Marilyn Isaacs examine the small silver-toned object. She was a woman of about sixty, with short gray hair, and bifocal glasses that rested low on her nose. There was an intelligence about Dr. Isaacs that David immediately trusted. Dr. Isaacs bent the object slightly, then scraped at it with her fingernail.

"Hmm . . ." she murmured.

David sat across a wooden desk from the professor.

Like most everything else at Oakdale College, the office had a time-worn, scholarly air that David liked. Wishbone sat obediently on the floor. For some reason, he had insisted on coming along.

Finally, Professor Isaacs looked at David over the lenses of her bifocals. "You're right, young man. This is puzzling. It seems to be made from some type of ceramic or clay-based material. But I've never seen a ceramic that could bend like this."

"Is there anyone else here at the college who might be able to identify it?" David asked.

"Probably so," the professor answered. "This isn't really my field of experience. If you'll allow me to keep this object, I'll show it to some of our other professors."

In addition to explaining how the object was found, David had also told Dr. Isaacs about his recent computer communication with someone or something claiming to be from another planet. Dr. Isaacs had listened patiently to the whole story with a slight smile on her lips.

"I read in the paper that you didn't know what caused the green glow," David mentioned. "Have you gotten any more information on that?"

Dr. Isaacs took off her bifocals and let them hang from a chain around her neck. "That glowing thing has got me stumped. It looked like an electrical phenomenon known as St. Elmo's fire, but that only happens during a lightning storm at sea. I've been on the phone all morning. I've spoken to astronomers, meteorologists, air-traffic controllers, none of whom can identify the glow. And I've spoken to several high-level government officials. All of them say the object was not of military origin."

David was amazed that none of those people could identify the mysterious green glow. "If you had to make a guess," he said, "what would you say it was?"

"I'd say it was just a very rare natural phenomenon. When you've been around as long as I have, you know Nature is always capable of surprising us."

David realized that Dr. Isaacs didn't seem to mind his taking up her time, so he figured he would get as much information as he could. "The so-called 'alien' who contacted me said it came from a planet that was nineteen light-years away. I know astronomers believe there are a lot of planets in the universe. But, except for the planets in our solar system, we don't really *know* of any other planets. Do we?"

The professor's eyes sparkled, making her suddenly appear many years younger. She said, "*Now* we do."

"Really?" David said.

"As you know," Dr. Isaacs explained, "planets revolve around stars. But since planets are much smaller than the stars they orbit, we've never been able to view any planets outside our solar system. But every day telescopes are improving. Just now, for the first time, astronomers are catching faint glimpses of planets beyond our solar system. And, yes, some of those planets are as close as nineteen light-years away."

David found this very interesting. "But those planets would not be able to . . . support life. Would they?"

Again the professor's eyes sparkled. "For years, biologists thought that planets capable of supporting life were very rare. They assumed life forms could live only on planets inside something known as a 'Goldilocks Zone.' This meant the planet's temperature must be just right. Not too hot, not too cold."

David knew something about this theory. "And this would depend on how close the planet was to the star it orbits," he said. "For example, Earth is just the right distance from its star, which is the sun. But Mercury and

Venus are too close to the sun, and the other planets in our solar system are too far away from it."

"Correct," Dr. Isaacs said. "Indeed, many biologists thought Earth might be the only planet in the entire universe that had the right temperature balance. At the very least, they thought the planets capable of supporting life would be scattered a great many light-years away from one another."

David was hanging on her every word. "But now?"

"New research," the professor explained, "has led biologists to believe that life, even intelligent life, may be able to live and grow in all sorts of environments. In other words, they may have been wrong about the Goldilocks Zone. And if they are, well, then, life may exist on a lot more planets than anyone realized before."

This was big news to David. Very big. "So, in fact," David said, "it's possible that there is intelligent life on a planet that's only nineteen light-years away from Earth?"

"It's . . . possible," Dr. Isaacs said. "Which doesn't mean that was an alien on your computer. It probably wasn't. Even so, I think you should keep quiet about your alien encounter. If you mention any of this to your parents or close friends, please ask them to be careful of what they say to others."

"Why is that?" David asked.

Dr. Isaacs locked her eyes on David. "Last night a very mysterious thing appeared in our skies. If word gets out about this silver object and your computer message, take my word for it, the alien rumors will start flying. It happens all the time in these types of situations. Before you know it, half the town will be heading for the hills. And the other half will be selling merchandise to all the UFO fanatics who won't be able to get here fast enough. Oakdale is a peaceful town. Let's try to keep it that way."

"I understand," David said.

"And you can count on me," Wishbone added. "I won't tell anyone about this, even if they bribe me with a year's supply of prime rib. Well, maybe not—"

Wishbone heard the sound of footsteps. The funny thing was, they seemed to be creeping away from the door to the professor's office. As David thanked Dr. Isaacs for her assistance, Wishbone walked to the door, which was partly open.

At once, he caught a familiar scent. It definitely wasn't prime rib, but Wishbone couldn't put a name to what it was. He slipped through the doorway and looked down the hallway. He saw a pair of shoes disappearing around a corner. Wishbone began to trot along the hallway's polished floor.

Behind him, Wishbone heard David appear in the hallway. "Hey, Wishbone," he called out, "you're going the wrong way."

"No, I'm not," Wishbone called back. "Follow me."

"Hey!" David said as he walked briskly after the dog. "Where's the fire?"

"There's no fire," Wishbone replied, "but I'm hot on the trail of someone who was listening to our conversation. Come on, let's high-tail it down the hall before this snooper escapes!"

Chapter Six

Wishbone hurried down the hallway, hearing the squeak of David's shoes following after him. Even though the hallway smelled mostly of cleaning ammonia and old building, Wishbone was able to follow the trail of the familiar scent. He realized it was a sweaty cotton smell, an odor he connected with someone he didn't completely trust.

Whoever this person was, Wishbone knew he or she would not be able to escape from his faithful black nose. The dog had tracked down many a rascal, human and otherwise, with the aid of this priceless detection device.

"I'm still not sure what you're doing," David called to Wishbone.

"You'll see soon enough," Wishbone called back.

Wishbone went toward a wooden door that smelled promising. But then he realized the fugitive had only briefly stopped at this door. Wishbone pressed ahead, soon stopping in front of another door. He gave a deep sniff under the crack.

Wishbone turned to David, who was right behind

him. "Yep, this is it—the door hiding the prize. Do you want me to open it, or would you like the honors for yourself?"

"Do you want me to open this?" David said as he grabbed the knob. He opened the door. It was a darkened broom closet. But standing in the middle of brooms, mops, and a variety of cleaning equipment was a person— Damont's cousin, Brewster Kidd. There was an embarrassed expression on his face, and he wore the same black T-shirt he had worn last night, the one announcing: "We will find the truth!"

"Yeah, that's what the smell was," Wishbone said to himself. "The T-shirt!"

"Brewster," David said with surprise, "what are you doing here?"

Brewster scratched his ear. "Oh, I was just . . . uh . . . doing some studying."

"In the broom closet?" Wishbone said. "Do you have a test coming up on janitorial supplies?"

"What were you studying?" David asked.

Brewster thought a moment. "Uh . . . tomorrow I have an astronomy exam. I go to this college, you know."

"Tomorrow is Sunday," David pointed out.

"Oh, that's right," Brewster said.

David narrowed his eyes. "Speaking of astronomy, I'm reminded of a certain constellation. It's called the Big Fibber. I think you were eavesdropping on my conversation with Dr. Isaacs. And you ducked in here because you heard me and Wishbone following you."

Brewster scratched his ear again. "Okay, Barnes, I'll come clean. I saw you walk into the building and I was curious to find out what you were up to. So I followed you and listened at the professor's door. I couldn't quite hear everything, though."

"What *did* you hear?" David and Wishbone asked at the same time.

Remaining in the closet, Brewster said, "For starters, I heard about that silver thing you found. And how you think it may have come from an alien spacecraft. But I didn't get a good look at it. What's it like, exactly? And can you describe that symbol?" There was now great interest showing on Brewster's face.

David released a sigh. "Since you listened to the conversation, you may have heard that Dr. Isaacs advised me to keep quiet about this. Sorry, but I'm not going to tell you anything, and neither is the professor."

"Oh, come on, man," Brewster pleaded. "The town I live in may be having an alien visitation. But I can't do anything about it unless I have a little more information!" Brewster gestured, accidentally flinging a paintbrush off a shelf.

"Uh . . . careful there, guy," Wishbone said, taking a cautious step back.

"We are *not* having an alien visitation," insisted David.

"Come on, this isn't the time to have a closed mind!" Brewster gestured again, this time sending a metal bucket and several plastic bottles crashing to the floor.

"Brewster," David said calmly, "it's because of people like you that the professor asked me to keep things quiet. If I were to tell you something, ten minutes later it would be on your Web site."

"And maybe it's time to come out of the broom closet," Wishbone suggested. "You're likely to hurt someone, including me."

A glare formed in Brewster's eyes. "This is just like Roswell!"

David was glad to see Brewster finally step out of the closet. Brewster knelt down to pick up the fallen items. With some amusement, David asked, "Why is this like Roswell?"

Brewster turned his head left, then right, to make sure the hallway was empty. David thought Brewster looked as if he were in a spy movie made on a very low budget.

"July—1947," Brewster whispered. "The desert of New Mexico. Right near the town of Roswell. One night, a sheep rancher sees a glowing form streak through the sky. The next morning, while walking across his land, the rancher finds a few pieces of a strange material. It's a silvery substance resembling foil, but it's very tough."

"I've heard about Roswell," David said. "What's your point?"

Brewster stood and returned the fallen items to the closet shelves. "The rancher calls the nearby army base," he continued. "Several military men show up at the ranch and take the objects away. Shortly afterward, the military issues a report that a mysterious material was found. But then, several hours later, a general announces to the public that the material came from a new kind of weather balloon. Obviously, the government changed its story, because it decided it didn't want people to know the truth." Brewster shut the closet door.

"Or maybe," David said, "the government was just being secretive because the objects really came from a floating espionage device—as the military admitted several years later."

Brewster grabbed David's shoulders. "Don't you see? That was just another phony story!"

Wishbone growled at Brewster. The college boy glanced nervously at the dog, then let go of David.

"Maybe it wasn't a phony story," David said, kneeling down to give Wishbone a grateful scratch.

Brewster knelt down to David's level and continued whispering. "There's more. That same day in 1947, a few miles from the sheep ranch, a civil engineer discovers a giant disk crashed into the ground. The disk is cracked open. Inside the disk lie several humanoid creatures with gray skin and big eyes. They're dead. The engineer notifies the military. Soon guarded army trucks come to cart away the wreckage and the bodies. That disk and those bodies are never seen or heard from again. Report has it that the military has been keeping them at an air force base out in Ohio. In a secret building known as Hangar Eighteen."

"As I recall," David said, standing up, "a few years ago, the government announced that those bodies were test dummies being used to check the effect of parachuting on humans."

"Don't you see?" Brewster said, also standing up. "It's more cover-up! What *really* happened that night near Roswell? I'll tell you what. Extraterrestrial beings crashed into the Earth. But for some reason, the government refuses to let us know about it. Now, I can't really do anything about that. But last night I think an extraterrestrial vehicle flew over my hometown. And I *will* discover the truth about that! Not just for myself, but for the world!"

"That's very generous of you," David remarked.

Brewster pointed an angry finger at David. "You *know* something, Barnes. And you're keeping your mouth shut. But I'll find the truth. Whatever it takes, I will find the truth! I'll see you tomorrow night, man. Live on the radio. Maybe you'll open your eyes between now and then!"

Brewster stalked away, his ponytail bouncing behind him. David almost felt some admiration for the guy. Brewster's beliefs were based mostly on rumor and unreliable sources, but he certainly had some passion behind those beliefs. At the same time, David felt there was something suspicious about Brewster. That may have been because he was caught snooping. Or it may have been because he was Damont's cousin. And nobody had more talent for stirring up trouble than Damont.

Chapter Seven

David turned to see Damont whizzing past him on a set of in-line skates. Damont executed a quick spin, then used his heel to bring himself to a stop. "Well, if it isn't the boy-wonder scientist," Damont said in a teasing tone.

David and Wishbone were standing on the sidewalk in front of Sam's house, where they had gone to meet up with Sam and Joe. Sam had the honor of living near Damont.

"How's it going?" David said with a small wave.

"Fine," Damont replied. "But it'll be going a lot better tomorrow night, when Brewster takes you down for the count on the radio show."

"It's a scientific discussion," David pointed out, "not a boxing match."

"We'll see about that," Damont said with a teasing grin. Then he whizzed off toward his house.

As David approached the Kepler house, he saw Sam and Joe standing in the front doorway. "I wonder if Damont will skate all the way to his room," Sam remarked.

Soon David, Joe, and Sam were gathered around the

dining room table of Sam's house. David smiled, thinking the trio looked like the Joint Chiefs of Staff discussing a matter of national security. Wishbone lay on the floor, but he seemed to have an ear cocked toward the conversation. Joe had already told Sam about the morning's events, and David brought them both up to date on what had happened at Oakdale College.

"So our mission is to prove that wasn't an alien contacting me," David told the others. "Now, if it wasn't an alien, that means it was somebody playing a trick. This raises the question of *who*?"

"Can you think of anyone who might have a reason for pulling this hoax on you?" Joe asked.

"Not really," David replied.

Sam was tapping a pencil on a sketch pad. "I can," she said. "Brewster."

"Why Brewster?" David asked. He was interested in Sam's opinion. Joe was a great athlete, and David was a science whiz, but when it came to human nature, Sam was the expert.

"Think about it," Sam said. "On the radio show, you're going to argue how unlikely the chances are of aliens visiting Earth. Brewster is going to argue that this type of event has happened many times. He knows you will be tough to beat. Maybe he's even afraid that you're smarter than he is. But if he's able to make you believe you're being contacted by an alien visitor . . ."

David nodded with understanding. "It'll throw me off. Either I'll cross over to his side of the fence, or, at the very least, the whole thing will weaken my opinion."

"Exactly," Sam said with a knowing look.

"That could make sense," David said thoughtfully. "This UFO thing is like a religion with Brewster. He seems desperate for people to believe that aliens have been visiting our planet. You should have seen the way he was going on about the Roswell incident."

"And if Brewster is behind this prank," Joe put in, "I'll bet Damont is helping him. Damont's always looking for an underhanded way to get the best of someone."

David held up a finger. "But what is that silver object, and how did Brewster or Damont get hold of it?"

"Yeah," Joe said, knitting his brow together. "And why did Brewster act so eager to know about the silver object? If he and Damont are the pranksters, then they would already know about it."

Sam twirled her pencil between her fingers. "Brewster Kidd might be more clever than we give him credit for. Maybe he figured if he did a good job pretending he didn't know about the object, it would *seem* as if he had nothing to do with it. And maybe he was eavesdropping on your conversation with the professor to see how well the prank was working."

"Okay," Joe said, "let's say Brewster and Damont *are* the culprits. Would they be able to do that computer trickery we saw this morning?"

"You're the computer expert," Sam said, gesturing at David.

David drummed his fingers on the table's surface. "I know Damont isn't that handy with a computer. But Brewster might be. He does have his own Web site. And from what I saw, it was fairly well designed. And the trickery wasn't really that complicated."

"How would someone do it?" Joe asked.

"If a person wants to go on the Internet, have an on-line conversation, or send some e-mail," David explained, "he or she has to go through a powerful computer system. Some businesses and universities have systems like this, but most people at home go through special companies called servers. The person who contacted me must have hacked his or her way into some off-limits area of my server—you know, found a sneaky way to enter the system. Once there, it would be easy to figure out how to operate a few things. It would take some basic knowledge of hacking. But not that much. I mean, there are probably eleven-year-old kids who could manage this sort of thing."

"Would there be any way to trace this person?" Sam asked. "The way the phone company can trace phone calls?"

"I've been thinking about that," David said. "As soon as we're done here, I'm going to see if I can create a trace program."

"But that will only help if the person contacts you again," Joe mentioned.

"Right," David replied. "But I'm pretty sure that'll happen. I get the feeling this person is planning to have plenty of laughs at my expense."

Joe looked at David. "Unless this person turns out to be a real alien."

Wishbone raised himself to a sitting position. "I was thinking the same thing myself, Joe. You know, guys, that reminds me. I heard this very low humming sound last night. I wonder if that could have been coming from an alien creature."

"It *wasn't* a real alien," David said to Joe.

"Yeah, you're probably right," Wishbone admitted. "If there was an alien in the neighborhood, I would have picked up its scent by now. My nose always knows what's going on."

Sam opened her sketch pad. "If E.T.s really existed, I wonder what they would look like."

"Impossible to say," David said, gazing into the distance. "That's the thing about extraterrestrial creatures. They are totally unknown to us in every way. I mean, they could look like *anything*. They could be as big as a skyscraper, or as small as an atomic particle. They might even live in a dimension we don't even know about."

"Hey, have you started to read *The War of the Worlds* yet?" Joe asked David.

"I couldn't put it down," David said. "Last night I got halfway through it."

"What do the aliens look like in the book?" Sam asked.

Wishbone gave the wooden floor an excited scratch. "Oh, I know! The creatures in *The War of the Worlds* are really some——"

"They're very scary," David said.

"Okay," Wishbone said, "since you're the one reading the book, I'll let you do the explaining."

David waved his arms in a snakelike fashion. "They're slimy, slithering creatures about the size of a bear. They have big eyes, and sixteen of these long, snake-like tentacles. And their brains are very powerful."

"How do they get around?" Joe asked.

"Well, you see," David explained, "the gravitational pull of Earth is a lot stronger than that of their native planet, Mars. That means their bodies feel extra heavy here on Earth. So they spend almost all their time in these machines they brought with them."

Wishbone noticed that Sam was sketching. Joe leaned forward and said, "What sort of machines?"

David walked his hands along the table in a robotic way. "There's this big metallic body that walks around on three long metallic legs. The whole thing is equal in height to a building several stories tall. And on top of the body is a headlike thing that can turn in all directions. And do you want to know the most frightening part?"

"Of course," Joe said.

Wishbone's ears were sticking straight up. "Are you kidding? We love 'frightening.' We live for 'frightening.' Uh . . . wait, just how frightening is this part?"

"There's a little funnel sticking out of the headlike thing," David said. "And it shoots out a heat ray."

"That's right," Wishbone said. "The heat ray!"

Sam looked up from her sketch pad. "What's a heat ray?"

"The heat ray," David said dramatically, "is an invisible beam that can shoot great distances. And whatever it touches immediately bursts into flames. You don't hear it or see it, but if it zaps you, well, you're history."

Sam made a face. "Not very comforting."

"How many of the Martians come to Earth?" Joe asked with interest.

"A whole mess of them," David replied. "Their plan is to take over the entire planet so they can live here themselves. Right now, they're moving through England, destroying everything in their path—trees, houses, buildings, and, of course, people. The military comes and shoots their biggest guns at the machines, but it doesn't have much effect. There doesn't seem to be any way to stop the Martians, and it looks like they'll—"

"Stop!" Joe exclaimed. "Don't tell me the ending! I've got to read this one."

"Relax, I won't," David said with a grin. "I haven't even gotten there yet."

"This reminds me of an old sci-fi movie my dad and I watched," Sam said as she continued to sketch. "But in

this movie, the aliens didn't travel in machines. They actually took over the bodies of human beings. The people whose bodies they were in still looked and talked the same. But the people were just a little different."

Wishbone lay back down on the floor. "Boy, those folks in Hollywood come up with the craziest ideas. Imagine, taking over the body of a human being. Of course, something like that could never really—"

A terrible thought zipped into Wishbone's mind. He dropped out of the conversation to think.

You know, maybe that idea isn't so crazy. Maybe that humming did come from an alien. But maybe I didn't smell the alien, because the alien was inside a familiar body. In a way, it makes perfect sense. Let's see, has anyone in the neighborhood shown highly unusual behavior since last night? No, I can't think of . . .

In his mind, Wishbone saw Wanda sitting in her chair—vibrating.

Hmmm . . . that low humming sound was loudest right near Wanda's house. Could an alien have taken over Wanda's body? Stranger things have happened. Well, no, actually that would be about as strange as it gets. I'd better not say anything to the others. Not yet, at least. No need to cause alarm.

"Ahhh!" Wishbone yelled in fright.

To his amazement, Wishbone saw an alien with big eyes and slithering tentacles sitting at the dining room table. Then he realized it was just a drawing on the sketch pad that Sam was holding up for the boys to see.

"Sam, please," Wishbone requested. "Don't scare us like that."

Chapter Eight

It was a spooky sort of night. Wishbone saw no stars or moon in the sky. There were only hazy white clouds floating through the blackness, as if they were ghostly intruders.

Wishbone was alone that night because Joe and Ellen were attending a fund-raising event at the library. Next door there was a light in Wanda's window, indicating she was home.

Wishbone walked across his front yard, heading straight for Wanda's house. As he approached, he heard the low humming sound.

He went to the front door and gave a scratch. There was no answer. He gave another scratch and called, "Hey, Wanda, open up! I need to borrow a cup of sugar!"

There was still no answer.

Wishbone trotted to the side of the house and climbed up on the bag of fertilizer. Through the window, he saw Wanda standing in the middle of her living room. She was in a very unusual position. Her hands were brought together in a praying gesture, and she was balancing on one foot. The other foot was elevated, its heel resting against the opposite leg.

Even stranger, Wanda wasn't moving a single muscle. Strangest of all, her eyes were glazed with an empty look that made her resemble a mannequin in a department store window.

What in the world is she doing? Wishbone thought.

Wishbone gave a scratch at the windowpane. But Wanda didn't budge.

"Hey!" Wishbone called. "I really need that cup of sugar!"

Wanda kept staring in the same eerie manner.

Wishbone gave another scratch. Wanda wasn't that far away, and she was facing the window. Wishbone was puzzled because he knew Wanda would have been able to hear the scratches . . . unless she was in some kind of a deep trance.

Could there be an alien living in Wanda's body? Wishbone wondered. *It's hard to tell. Let's face it. Wanda is always a little strange. But I really think she's acting way more strange than usual. I don't like this. No, sir, I don't like it one teeny bit. I need some advice on this. Who can I talk to? I know. David!*

Wishbone jumped down from the fertilizer bag and trotted over to the Barneses' house. After the dog gave a few scratches, the front door was opened by David's seven-year-old sister, Emily. She stood there in a white nightgown. Most people found Emily adorable, but she made Wishbone a little nervous.

"Oh, it's Wishbone!" Emily cried out with delight. She crouched down to rub the dog's head.

"Hi, Emily," Wishbone replied. "Uh . . . . careful there. Remember, no funny stuff with the ears."

"Did you come to play with me?" Emily asked.

"Actually," Wishbone informed the girl, "I came to see David about a security matter. Thanks for letting me in, though."

Wishbone scampered past Emily, went upstairs, and headed straight for the door of David's room.

After all these years, David knew Wishbone's scratch. From his seat at the desk, David pressed a button on his remote-control door-opening device. The door buzzed. Wishbone nudged the door open with his muzzle, shut the door the same way, then walked into the room. David was surprised to see Wishbone had come without Joe.

"I'm getting pretty popular with you, aren't I?" David said. "Oh, that's right. Joe and his mom went to that thing at the library. You were probably just lonely."

Wishbone looked up at David, his brown eyes glowing. It was almost as if the dog was trying to tell David something of great importance.

"Is something wrong?" David asked with concern.

Wishbone gave a bark.

The phone jingled. David swiveled to it and picked up the receiver. "Hello," he said.

"May I speak to David Barnes?" a voice said.

David recognized the voice. "Hi, Dr. Isaacs. This is David. Did you find out anything?"

"No, I didn't," Dr. Isaacs replied. "I showed that object to two other professors here at the college—our chemistry and engineering experts. Neither of them could identify the material."

"That's very odd, isn't it?" David asked.

"Yes, it is," Dr. Isaacs said. "This leads me to believe it might be some kind of experimental material. I've sent it off to a scientist I know who works at the research laboratory of a large corporation. If anyone can identify this thing, he's the one. But it might be a couple of days before I hear any news from him. As soon as I do, I'll let you know."

"Okay, thanks," David said.

Dr. Isaacs said, "Have a nice night."

David hung up the receiver and thought a moment. He was puzzled that neither a chemistry nor engineering expert could identify the material.

Wishbone, who had been waiting politely throughout the phone call, now gave another bark at David.

David swiveled to the dog. "I wish I could understand what you want. But I can't. I'm really sorry."

A musical chime sounded from David's computer. David swiveled to look at the screen, which showed information from a UFO Web site. David had been staying on-line in the event that the prankster returned.

The screen turned pitch-black. Then the word "Hello" appeared in fluorescent green letters.

David knew it was a visit from the on-line alien.

Wishbone nudged David's leg.

"I know, I know," David said, as he lifted Wishbone into the chair beside him. "You like a front-row seat for the show."

Wishbone stared at the screen, as if he knew exactly what was going on. At the keyboard, David typed the words: "Hello. I am glad to hear from you again."

The words appeared on the screen in fluorescent purple. As he did that morning, David hit the "Return" key and the words turned fluorescent green, signaling the message had been sent.

While he waited for the next message to come, David inserted a diskette in the disk drive. Then he tapped a command key to start it. The disk contained a trace program David had spent most of the afternoon creating with a special computer language. He knew the program would take about a minute to work.

This message came from the alien: "I am still watching you."

As before, the messages began scrolling upward.

David typed and sent: "Can you tell me now why you're watching me?"

Before an answer came, a white rectangle appeared in the upper right of David's screen. This was part of his trace program. The program would go to the server, find the screen name of the party who was sending the messages, and then the screen name would appear in the box. Once David had the screen name, it would be easy enough to find the person's real name. David had tested the program with Lisa, one of his computer buddies, and it worked very well.

This message came back: "I'm watching you for this reason. I want you to tell other humans about me. As many humans as you can possibly reach. And I want you to do it tomorrow."

David found this an interesting request. He sent: "Why me?"

This returned: "You seem like a highly intelligent messenger."

David sent: "Well, thanks for the compliment! Why tomorrow?"

This returned: "So the humans of the world will be prepared."

David sent: "Prepared for what?"

This returned: "I cannot reveal that information."

Even though David knew this was just a game, the last two responses left him feeling uncomfortable.

Something appeared in the white rectangle. But it wasn't a screen name. It was a phone number with an area code. Before David could grab a pen to write down the phone number, the number changed. Then it changed again. Again and again. Then phone numbers began flying by faster and faster; the area codes came from all over the country. The numbers began spinning by so fast, they turned into a meaningless blur.

"Darn!" David said under his breath. He realized the party communicating with him had anticipated the trace program and had used a program to battle it. David tapped a key to deactivate the program.

Okay, David thought. *Don't get discouraged. There has to be more than one way to catch a person operating under the alias of an alien. Maybe I can trip him or her up with some tricky questions.*

David sent: "I'm curious about the craft that brought you to my planet. How fast does it travel?"

David figured that this question might trip up an impostor, especially if it was Brewster.

This returned: "It can increase up to the speed of light. Nothing in the universe can go beyond that speed."

Well, he got that one right, David thought.

David sent: "I know. I was trying to explain that to someone named Brewster yesterday, but he didn't believe me."

This returned: "Oh."

David sent: "How long did it take you to reach Earth?"

This returned: "Since the distance between our worlds is about nineteen light-years, the journey took a little over nineteen years. The majority of the time the craft was traveling at top speed. And for me, nineteen years is not very long. My species has a life expectancy of two hundred and ten years."

If the alien's planet is nineteen light-years away, the math is right, David thought. *So far the alien is doing fairly well. Even if it is Brewster.*

David thought up another tactic and sent: "Where did you learn English?"

This returned: "On my planet we have picked up radio waves coming from your planet. We have translated them into sound. In the case of television, which also travels through radio waves, we have translated the sound and the pictures."

David sent: "So you learned to speak English through radio and television programs?"

This returned: "Yes. I have also learned other Earth languages in this manner."

So far, so good, David thought. He knew what the alien was saying was actually possible. He was aware that for years scientists had been wondering if aliens might be picking up broadcasts from Earth. Indeed, David knew that some astronomers worked in a program known as

SETI, or Search for Extra-Terrestrial Intelligence. Using huge radio telescopes, these astronomers listened for radio waves that might be coming from intelligent creatures on distant planets. David realized, of course, that Brewster knew all about the radio-wave thing.

David sifted through his brain for something that would really stump the alien. He sent: "Do you have any favorite radio or TV programs from Earth?"

This was an especially tricky question. Because radio waves traveled at the speed of light, David knew the alien's planet could not have received any program broadcast more recently than nineteen years ago. And if the alien had been traveling for the past nineteen years, it would not be familiar with any program broadcast more recently than thirty-eight years ago.

This returned: "*I Love Lucy.*"

"Darn again!" David said, slapping the desk in frustration. David knew that *I Love Lucy* was originally broadcast more than forty years ago. As funny as it seemed, it was possible that extraterrestrial creatures living on a distant planet could be watching the comic adventures of Lucy, Ricky, Fred, and Ethel.

David sent: "How is it that you are communicating with me? Are you using a computer?"

This returned: "No, I am not using a computer. Only the power of my mind."

David considered this. He had read how the Martians in *The War of the Worlds* communicated with one another only through their brains. And he knew that some humans were supposedly capable of the same communication process—mental telepathy. Using the mind to put words on a screen was a different matter. But perhaps it wasn't impossible to do.

David decided he would come up with other questions

that might lead the alien into making a mistake. He sent: "Why have you come here?"

This returned: "I cannot reveal that information."

David sent: "Did you come here all alone, or with others?"

This returned: "I cannot reveal that information."

David sent: "Are you planning to stay on Earth?"

This returned: "I cannot reveal that information."

Well, David thought, *it looks like the alien is getting tired of coming up with the perfect answers.*

David sent: "Will any of this information ever be revealed?"

This returned: "Yes. Very soon. Good-bye."

All the green words faded, signaling the on-line alien had signed off. The pitch-blackness gave way to the information on the Web site David had been visiting.

David rested his chin on his hand, thinking. He had to admit the alien impostor was proving to be a worthy opponent. Not only had the alien done a good job of answering David's questions and foiling the trace program, but it had supplied a material that not even experts at the college could identify. Of course, the person could not have been responsible for the mysterious green glow. Not unless . . .

As David sat there, his thoughts became haunted by a very troubling question. *Have I been communicating with a fellow human traveling through cyberspace? Or is it possible— just maybe possible—that I've been communicating with an intelligent being from* outer space?

David became aware of a dim sound, the television set in his parents' bedroom. David had not told them anything about the on-line alien. He would do so, but . . . not yet. He felt like calling Joe or Sam, but he knew both of them were out for the evening.

David looked at Wishbone, who was still sitting in the chair beside him. Feeling the need for contact with someone friendly and familiar, he stroked Wishbone's back. The dog's presence gave him a sense of comfort.

"What do you say we do a little reading?" David told Wishbone. "We'll go see Joe as soon as we hear his mom's Explorer drive up."

David went to his bed and stretched out. Wishbone jumped down from the chair and reclined right beside the bed.

David opened *The War of the Worlds* and reentered the story. By this point, the Martians had destroyed most of England with their powerful heat rays. Thousands of people had been killed. Those remaining had stampeded through the streets of the cities and fled through the countryside. As David read on, England became overrun with a blood-red weed the Martians had brought from their native planet. The human race was facing complete doom.

On any night, David would have found the book scary. But recent events made the story seem ten times more frightening than it would have been any other time.

As Wishbone watched David read, he kept his senses on full alert. He needed to be ready for anything that night. He was frustrated David didn't really pay any attention to his theory about Wanda, but he figured that was because David had a lot of other things on his mind.

A breeze rolled in through the open window. Wishbone heard the gentle sounds of a spring evening and, off in the distance, the low humming sound.

After a few minutes, Wishbone saw David shudder in reaction to something he had read. David looked over at Wishbone and said, "Listen, boy. If some slimy creature with tentacles tries to get into the house, you'll give me a warning, won't you?"

Wishbone glanced up at David with a look of confidence. "That's what I'm here for, old friend. I am the neighborhood chief of security!"

Chapter Nine

The sun glowed with warmth in a pure blue sky. Sunday was normally Wishbone's day of leisure, but this great morning on the planet Earth, he had a very serious mission. He stood in his front yard, looking across the driveway at Wanda's house.

As soon as Joe and Ellen had returned home the night before, Wishbone revealed his suspicions about Wanda. But Joe and Ellen had paid no more attention to this information than David had. Nevertheless, Wishbone knew he must find out whether or not Wanda had been taken over by an alien. He had to do it that very hour. Even if it meant doing the job alone.

"Wish me luck," Wishbone told himself.

Then, with a firm stride, Wishbone headed over to Wanda's house. He went straight for the fertilizer bag, climbed to the top, found the window open, and jumped through.

Wishbone landed on his padded paws as silently as possible. Then his sharp eyes swept around the living room. He saw the flower-print wallpaper, the old-fashioned furniture, the hanging glass beads, the collection of modern artwork, and all the other neat stuff Wanda kept around.

The place looked the same way it usually did. But Wishbone was picking up something bizarre—a bitter, burning, cinnamon-like scent. Wishbone followed his nose to a coffee table, where he saw a skinny stick in a little stand. A steady stream of smoke drifted up from the stick's tip.

What's the story with this? Wishbone wondered. *Could that stick be releasing a smell that reminds the alien of its native planet? That must be it. Why else would someone want that smelly aroma in their house?*

Feeling a hand on his back, Wishbone jerked around.

Wanda was standing over him. She wore a flowing pink robe decorated with lots of funny shapes. "Well, isn't this a surprise," Wanda said with great cheer. "I guess you climbed in through the window."

Wishbone took a seat on the floor, doing his best to act casual. "Uh . . . that's right. You know, I got to thinking. I spend a lot of time in Wanda's yard but I almost never come pay a visit inside her lovely house. Like any good neighbor should. So . . . here I am."

"I'm glad you dropped in," Wanda said. "Do make yourself comfortable." Wanda walked to a chair, took a seat, and began filing her fingernails. For the most part, she was acting perfectly natural. Except maybe she was being just a bit nicer than usual. She was also holding her back kind of stiff and straight.

Across the room, something caught Wishbone's eye—a small purple rock that rested on a windowsill. A beam of sunlight shone through the rock, revealing it to be clear and almost magically glowing.

What's the deal with that? Wishbone wondered.

Doesn't look like any of the rocks I've come across on my many digging expeditions. No, sir, I'm pretty sure that thing is from another galaxy far, far away. I'll bet it sends off an energy force that feeds into the alien's brain. Better not get too close.

Wanda began humming as she filed her nails.

"So, Wanda," Wishbone said in an offhand way, "how the heck have you been?"

Wanda kept humming and filing.

"Have you been feeling all right?" Wishbone asked.

Wanda gave no answer.

"The reason I ask is this," Wishbone continued, "you don't seem to be . . . quite yourself these days. If you catch my meaning."

Wanda glanced at Wishbone but said nothing.

"Listen," Wishbone said in a more serious manner, "I know you and I have had our differences. Sometimes you think I'm damaging your beautiful flowers, and every now and then I suspect you may have done a little gnawing on one of my bones. But these are small details. And if there's anything you want to talk about . . . anything you want to get off your chest or . . . out of your *body* . . . well . . . I'm here for you."

Wanda bounced to her feet and hurried toward the kitchen. "Oh, I almost forgot—it's time for my dose of nutrition!"

Wanda wants to talk to me, Wishbone thought as he watched Wanda disappear. *I can tell. But the alien inside her body won't allow it. Now that the alien has had some time to practice, it's doing a better job of imitating her. But I'm not fooled. Not for a single second. Alas, it's true. Poor Wanda has been taken over by an extraterrestrial mind!*

Wanda returned to her chair, now holding a plate on her lap. Wishbone climbed onto a nearby footstool to have a look. On the plate there was a cube of something looking like a soft white clay. Wishbone craned his neck toward the plate and then took a sniff. The white clay had almost no smell.

I know where this stuff came from, Wishbone thought. *That little convenience store located just down the street from Neptune. You know, I bet it's a drug that robs Wanda of the will to resist her alien invader.*

"Would you like a bite?" Wanda asked politely.

"Uh . . . no, thanks," Wishbone replied.

Wanda sliced off a piece of the white clay with a fork, stuck it in her mouth, and chewed happily. After swallowing, she said, "This is one of the healthiest things a person can eat."

"I'm sure it is," Wishbone said, "but I just had a box of kibble before I came over here. I ate the whole thing. Including the box itself."

Wanda leaned over to Wishbone and smiled. "It's all right if you take a bite. Really, it is. I saw you sniffing, so I know you're interested."

Wishbone pulled back his head. "I said no."

Wanda leaned closer. "I could put some in a bowl for you."

Wishbone jumped down from the footstool. *I'd better beat it,* he thought. *The alien inside Wanda is really trying to get some of that junk into my mouth. And, for all I know, any second this thing might pull out some dangerous intergalactic weapon.*

Wishbone darted across the room and used a chair to climb onto the windowsill. He looked right at Wanda, hoping he might be able to get a message to the *real* her. "Wanda Gilmore, I'll find a way to save you. I promise. Hang in there. In the meantime, do me a favor. Try not to eat too much of that stuff."

Wishbone leaped out the window and didn't stop running until he was on the grass of his own yard. He realized every bit of fur on his back was bristling.

This is a nightmare, Wishbone thought with a racing heart. *An evil-minded alien is living inside the body of Wanda. Action must be taken. But I'm not sure I can do this alone. Who can I call on for assistance? Who will understand?*

Wishbone sat down to collect his thoughts.

What can I do? What can . . . I know. Tonight I'll go to the radio station with David and explain the whole thing on the air. Surely there must be someone out there listening who will know how to handle a situation like this. At least, I hope there is. Otherwise, we may have a national disaster on our hands!

Wishbone turned his head toward David's house.

Wow! I smell a delicious breakfast cooking over there.

Chapter Ten

As David entered the kitchen, he was greeted by the tempting smells of scrambled eggs, bacon, and toast. David's mom and dad were setting out breakfast on the table, and Emily was giggling over some of the comics in the Sunday paper.

"Somebody was up mighty late last night," Mrs. Barnes said, as she picked up a carton of orange juice." David's mom was an attractive woman with long black hair. She accepted her son's unusual projects with good humor, at least most of the time.

"I guess you saw my light on," David said, as he took a seat at the table. "But I had some really important stuff to talk to Joe and Sam about on the phone. Then I got so caught up in *The War of the Worlds*, I had to finish it."

"Hey, tonight's the big night," Mr. Barnes said, as he set a plate of hot food in front of David. "My son makes his radio debut." David's dad was a well-built man with a moustache. He was kind of on the cool side, even if he was a parent.

Mr. and Mrs. Barnes joined the kids at the table. "I was thinking we should invite everyone over to listen to the broadcast," Mrs. Barnes told her husband. "Ellen, Joe, Wanda, Sam, Walter Kepler, if he can get away from the restaurant. We could serve a nice supper."

"Sounds great," Mr. Barnes said, as he spooned sugar into his coffee mug.

Emily looked up from the comics and said, "Can Wishbone come, too?"

"If there's food," Mrs. Barnes remarked, "I'm sure Wishbone will make an appearance."

Everyone at the table laughed. David was pleased to have his family around him that morning. He had spent a difficult night, haunted by dreams of terrifying alien creatures invading his hometown. Each time David awoke from one of those dreams he found himself wondering if the dream might soon become a reality. The worst part was that David's fears had not completely vanished with the rising of the sun.

David looked around the table at his family. *Is there a chance that there could be an alien lurking nearby?* he wondered. *A creature as deadly as the ones in* The War of the Worlds? *A creature who might try to harm my family and my friends?*

As David picked up a piece of bacon, he wondered whether he should mention his conversations with the alien tonight on the radio show. He figured quite a few people would be listening. Maybe a listener who knew more about those things would call and offer advice. Perhaps this person could determine if there was a threat, and, if so, suggest how to deal with it. David was still pretty sure the alien was *not* real, but, then, again . . .

Mr. Barnes tapped David on the arm. "David, did you hear what I just said?"

"Uh . . . no," David said. "Sorry, I was thinking about something."

"I asked if you knew that there was a very famous radio dramatization of *The War of the Worlds*."

"No, I didn't."

"Matter of fact, I wrote a paper on it in college."

"Why was it so famous?" David asked, as he lifted a forkful of scrambled eggs to his mouth.

David saw that glimmer in his dad's eyes that told him a story was coming. That was okay, because his dad told great tales. And some of them were true.

"That was in 1938," Mr. Barnes began. "Back in those days, of course, people didn't have TVs or computers, so radio programs were the main source of home entertainment. And there was this drama group called the Mercury Theatre. Every week the members would perform an adaptation of some classic story on the air."

Emily was finding this story even better than the funnies. "How can people perform on the radio?" she asked.

"They had to do all the acting with their voices," Mrs. Barnes explained.

"That's right," Mr. Barnes continued. "And the lead actor for the Mercury Theatre was this terrific young actor with a very deep voice. His name was Orson Welles. He was also one of the producers of the show."

"He wasn't related to H. G. Wells, was he?" David asked his dad.

"No," Mr. Barnes said. "It was just a coincidence that they had similar names."

After another bite of eggs, David said, "I still don't understand why the radio adaptation of *The War of the Worlds* was so famous."

Mr. Barnes buttered a slice of toast. "Because the actors in the Mercury Theatre group made it seem like an actual alien invasion *was* taking place—for real. They updated the story to 1938, and they set it in New Jersey instead of

England. Then they did the whole show in the form of a live news report."

"But didn't they announce at the beginning that it was just a dramatization?" David asked.

Mr. Barnes added some jam to his toast. "Yes, they did. But, you see, Orson Welles was a very clever showman. He knew that most folks didn't listen to his show from the beginning. Most folks started out listening to another show on a different station. The other show was a lot more popular."

"What was the other show about," Emily asked brightly.

"You may not believe this," Mr. Barnes said, "but it featured a famous man who did a ventriloquist act."

Emily looked puzzled. "What's a ventriloquist act?"

"That's when the entertainer has a big wooden puppet," Mrs. Barnes explained, "and he makes it seem like the puppet is actually talking."

Total confusion showed on Emily's face. "How can a puppet look like it's talking if it's just on the radio!"

After a bite of toast, Mr. Barnes said, "I don't know. But my father claimed it was the funniest show he ever heard. Anyway, most everyone would tune in for the ventriloquist act. But after that act was over, a lot of people would change stations to find out what was on the Mercury Theatre program."

"Like switching channels with the remote control," Emily said, proud that she understood that part.

"I see," David said with a nod. "So those people switched over during the middle of *The War of the Worlds*. They hadn't heard the announcement that this was just a dramatic presentation. They thought it was a *real* newscast reporting about Martians landing in New Jersey."

"You got it," Mr. Barnes said.

"Did it scare people?" Emily asked.

Mr. Barnes opened his eyes wide. "Boy, did it! When people heard that news broadcast about Martians landing on Earth and shooting things with something called a heat ray, well . . . panic broke out."

David leaned forward with interest. "What sort of panic?"

Mr. Barnes gestured for extra effect. "Police phone lines were flooded. Some people ran into the streets, screaming. Others rushed into the nearest church to pray. Roads and highways along the East Coast were jammed with cars filled with people trying to get away. And a few people were even hospitalized from shock. A lot of folks thought it was the end of the world!"

"I think I can understand," David said thoughtfully. "The story is really scary." He didn't explain just how true that statement was to him personally.

Emily set down her fork and declared, "Norton Wills shouldn't have scared all those people."

Mrs. Barnes smiled. "That's *Orson Welles*, honey."

"Well," Emily said, "he shouldn't have done it. Did he get in trouble?"

"You're right, Emily, he should not have done it," Mr. Barnes said after a sip of coffee. "And, no, he didn't get into trouble. But, the fact is, the program made him famous overnight. For weeks, everyone was talking about Orson Welles and his incredible *War of the Worlds* hoax. The Mercury Theatre became the hottest radio show on the air, and Orson Welles got a contract to write, direct, and star in Hollywood movies."

Mrs. Barnes pointed a finger at David. "But don't get any ideas in your head," she said playfully. "Your father and I don't want you starting a nationwide panic tonight. Besides, we won't let you go to Hollywood until *after* you finish college."

David laughed, but the Orson Welles story had got him thinking. He was willing to bet that Gilbert Pickering knew about the famous 1938 broadcast. After all, *The War of the Worlds* was one of Gilbert's favorite books. He wondered if Gilbert could be the one behind the alien hoax. The alien wanted David to tell a lot of people about its existence, and wanted it done today. Maybe Gilbert was trying to trick David into speaking about the on-line alien on the air—as a way of stirring up some buzz to publicize his show.

But then David realized that wasn't a likely theory. If Gilbert wanted to trick a guest into believing there was an alien, hoping that the guest would talk about it on the show, David would be a poor choice. In fact, David would probably be the last person in Oakdale to swallow that kind of bait. And Gilbert would know that.

As David chewed a piece of toast, he realized something else. A very good reason why he should not say anything on the air about the on-line alien was the way people reacted to the 1938 *War of the Worlds* broadcast. He might start another alien panic.

David decided the best thing to do was to keep trying to prove the alien was not real. It would be great if he could do that before the radio broadcast. He felt there was an excellent chance the alien would show up again that day. Now he needed to think of a really sneaky trap to lay for the alien.

David realized his mom had just asked him a question. "I'm sorry, Mom," he said. "What did you say?"

"I've never read *The War of the Worlds*," Mrs. Barnes told him. "I'm curious to know who wins the war—the humans or the Martians?"

"Well, it looks like the Martians are going to win," David said, as he gathered some egg on his fork. "They're destroying people left and right with their heat rays, and there doesn't seem to be any way to stop them. But then something very lucky happens. You see, there are all sorts of bacteria germs on Earth. Most of these germs don't bother humans and other animals because our bodies are used to them. But the Martians aren't used to these germs. They get infected by the bacteria, and before long they all die."

"I see," Mrs. Barnes said. "So, it's like they catch a really bad case of the flu or pneumonia that would not kill humans, but it would certainly kill the Martian invaders."

"That's right," David said after a bite of eggs.

David heard his fork clatter on the floor. It had slipped from his hand as a fantastic idea jumped into his mind. *The Martians in* The War of the Worlds *were stopped by bacteria. Which is similar to a virus. And maybe I can catch the on-line alien with a* computer virus!

David sprang to his feet. "Uh . . . Mom, Dad, may I be excused? I'm pretty full, and I thought of something really important I have to take care of."

"Sure, son," Mr. Barnes said with a confused look. "But what's the rush?"

David picked up the fork and set it on the table. "I need to go fight an alien!"

Chapter Eleven

Wishbone saw a humanlike creature with smooth skin and a really big head lying on an operating table. It was a photograph on the screen of David's computer. Below the picture was the caption: "Photo of deceased alien reportedly taken at Hangar 18."

David sat in front of the computer. He had called Sam and Joe a little while ago and asked them to come over. They stood on one side of David; and Wishbone, who had also come over, sat in a chair on the other side of him. The group was hooked into Brewster's Web site, waiting for the alien to cut in for another visit.

"That E.T. looks kind of cute," Sam said with a smile. "Phony, but cute."

"It looks like a phony to me, too," Wishbone put in. "But I'm telling you, guys, the alien who sent the silver thing is real. And it's living inside Wanda's body." No one responded. "Nope, looks like you still don't believe me."

"Where's the virus?" Joe asked David.

David tapped a key, and a diskette ejected from his computer. "Right there. I've been working on it for the past few hours. Just before you guys came over, I gave it a

trial run. I sent it to my computer buddy, Lisa, and it worked like a charm."

Sam and Joe looked at the diskette, while Wishbone gave it a good sniff.

"How does it work?" Sam asked.

"When the alien contacts me," David explained, "I'll send it the virus through the phone lines. Even though the alien won't know I'm sending it, the virus will be in his computer."

"Don't viruses usually cause a whole mess of damage?" Joe said.

David pushed the diskette back into the disk drive. "Not this one. It's designed to do one thing only. When I find the infected computer, I'll type in a special code, and the words 'I am watching you' will appear on the screen. The virus won't affect or damage anything on the system. It's just a way for me to identify the computer that is being used to send all of these alien messages."

"What's the special code?" Joe asked.

"3-8-H-O-A-X," David said with some pride. "That's because that radio hoax I was telling you about took place in 1938."

"Oh, very nice code," Wishbone said.

Sam walked around the room, thinking. "But, then, the only way this virus will work is if you know whose computer to check, right?"

"Right," David said.

"*If* the messages are coming from a computer, and not a real alien," Joe said.

"For a little while," David admitted, "I was beginning to believe in the alien myself. But I'm back to being certain it's a fake. And the more I think about it, the more I think Brewster must be the culprit."

"Why?" Sam asked, sitting on David's bed.

"This has turned into quite a prank," David said. "And I can't see anyone doing that unless they are out to get me for some reason."

"You mean someone has a bone to pick," Wishbone offered.

"But why?" David asked. "Who would be out to get me?"

"Does anyone have a grudge against you for any reason?" Joe asked.

David gave a shrug. "I've been wracking my brain. The only person I could think of was Brent Arnold. In third grade, I told the teacher that he was teasing the classroom hamster. Brent was pretty mad at me for a long time."

"Well, I am glad you busted him," Wishbone said. "Hamsters have constitutional rights, too, you know. Or at least they should."

A musical chime sounded at the computer. Wishbone felt his whiskers twitch with excitement.

91

Immediately, everybody gathered in front of the screen.

David watched the screen turn pitch-black. Then the word "Hello" appeared in fluorescent green.

"It's him," David said in a low voice.

"Or her," Sam suggested.

"Or it," Joe added.

David felt a buzz in his fingertips. He knew it was the excitement of a detective about to lay his hands on a criminal. As David typed on his keyboard, he said, "Okay, I'm starting the virus."

"How long will it be until the virus infects the other computer?" Joe asked.

"According to my trial run," David said, "we should give it a full four minutes."

Joe looked at his watch. "So you need to keep him, her, or it talking for four minutes. I'll keep track of the time."

David typed the following sentences: "Hello. Why are you contacting me again?"

The words appeared in fluorescent purple. When David tapped the "Return" key, the words then changed to fluorescent green.

"Nice colors," Sam observed.

A few moments later, the following message came back in green: "I must remind you of your mission to inform other humans about me. As many as you are able to reach. Remember, today is the day that I want this done."

As before, the messages began scrolling upward. Out of the corner of his eye, David noticed that Wishbone was watching the screen very closely.

"This is kind of creepy," Sam murmured.

Joe kept his eyes focused on his watch.

David typed and sent: "Why do you want this done today?"

A moment later, a message returned: "I cannot reveal this information."

David sent: "Why not?"

This returned: "I cannot reveal this information. I must go now. I am using most of my mental energy to communicate with others of my race. We are planning something of great importance. Good-bye."

"Don't let him go!" Sam exclaimed.

David quickly typed and sent: "Wait!"

This returned: "Yes?"

"Just under two and a half minutes remaining," Joe said.

David typed and sent: "What are you planning?"

This returned: "I cannot reveal this information."

"Two minutes left," Joe said.

Keep it going! David thought. *Keep it going!*

David sent: "What do you look like?"

This returned: "I cannot reveal this information."

David sent: "Why not?"

This returned: "I cannot reveal this information."

"Ninety seconds," Joe said.

David felt sweat forming on his forehead. He sensed that the alien would be signing off any second, before the virus could take hold. For a moment, David couldn't think of what to ask next.

"Ask if it looks like a human being," Sam said.

David sent: "Do you look like a human?"

This returned: "No."

"Sixty seconds," Joe said.

David realized he was holding his breath.

David sent: "Do you breathe oxygen?"

This returned: "Yes, either from the air or the water."

"Thirty seconds," Joe said.

David started to type a question, but then he panicked and forgot what it was. His mind went blank. "Sam, help me out!" he said in desperation. "What should I say next?"

"Uh . . . uh . . ." Sam stammered. "I can't . . ."

"Come on!" Joe urged. "Send something!"

David sent: "What is your favorite episode of *I Love Lucy?*"

This returned: "The one where Lucy is stomping grapes."

"This is *sooo* weird," Sam remarked.

"Time is . . . up!" Joe cried out triumphantly.

David let out a big sigh.

Then he realized that the alien had not yet signed off. As David stared at the green letters on the screen, a new question entered his mind. Even though David did not really believe the alien was real, he needed an answer.

David sent: "Have you come to Earth in peace or in war?"

A long moment passed.

This returned: "I cannot reveal this information. Good-bye."

As the green letters faded, David felt a chill rising up his spine. *If the alien is real*, David wondered, *could it be planning an invasion of Earth? If so, what would be the result of such a war? It wouldn't be like fighting against a foreign country. It would be fighting the . . . unknown.* David continued to stare at the screen, watching the blackness give way to the gray humanoid creature on the operating table.

"Wow!" Sam said softly. "I didn't think I was going to fall for this. But when the alien was sending those answers, suddenly I got this totally queasy feeling in my stomach. Like maybe, just maybe, it *is* the real thing."

"I'm glad to hear you say that," Joe said to Sam. "Because that's exactly how I felt both times I watched David talking to it."

David forced his eyes away from the screen. He swiveled to the phone and picked up the receiver. "Let's just keep trying to prove this alien isn't real." As he began to dial a number, he noticed that Wishbone was watching his every move.

"Who are you calling?" Joe asked.

"First, Damont," David said. "Even though Brewster's the computer expert, they could be using Damont's computer. I'll put the call on speakerphone."

David hit a button on the phone.

After two rings, a female voice came through the speaker. "Hello?"

"Hi, Mrs. Jones," David said, keeping his voice casual. "This is David Barnes. Is Damont there?"

"No, he's not," Mrs. Jones replied. "He's out skating around somewhere. May I take a message?"

"That's not necessary," David said. "But, thanks."

David pressed the hang-up button, then dialed the number for Oakdale College. He asked to be connected to Brewster's dorm room.

"Are you calling Brewster?" Sam asked.

David nodded. A moment later, a busy signal sounded through the phone speaker.

David hung up the receiver. "Brewster could be talking on the phone," he said. "But there's a chance he just has one phone line and it's busy because he's now using it to get on-line. But we can be pretty sure he's in his dorm room."

"So what do we do now?" Joe asked.

"We go to Brewster's dorm and check his computer for the virus," David explained. "This is the tricky part."

"What if he doesn't let us check?" Sam asked.

David rolled his chair back and stood up. "That's why it's the tricky part."

Chapter Twelve

"Everybody just follow my lead," Wishbone advised. "Operation Brewster is under way. They don't call me Commando Dog for nothing!"

Wishbone was guiding David, Joe, and Sam along a walkway that led through the grassy campus of Oakdale College. Most of the college buildings were old, with ivy crawling along their red-brick walls. Wishbone saw a squirrel dart up a tree trunk, but he resisted the temptation to give chase.

"That's Brewster's dorm," David told his friends, pointing toward a nearby building.

Behind the group, Wishbone heard something whizzing noisily along the concrete walkway. Everyone turned to see Damont skid to a quick stop on his in-line skates.

"Uh-oh," Wishbone said under his breath.

"Hey, what are you guys doing here?" Damont asked in his hot-shot way. "The last time I looked, all of you were just in eighth grade."

"What are *you* doing here?" Sam asked Damont.

"I'm going to visit my cousin, Brewster," Damont

said. "I want to make sure he's in top condition for the radio show tonight."

"Are you his manager?" Joe asked.

"Sort of," Damont said. "So, anyway, where are you guys going?"

"Uh . . . well . . ." David said, "we were going to Brewster's dorm, too. We wanted to . . . uh . . . wish him good luck."

Wishbone felt himself wince. David's words didn't come out very convincingly, and Damont obviously wasn't buying them.

"I don't believe you, Barnes," Damont said. "You guys are up to something, but I'm not sure what."

Wishbone could see there was a hundred-and-fifty-pound stumbling block in the way of the operation—Damont. Now that he was suspicious, he would probably go to Brewster's room and warn him. This would make it even more difficult to check Brewster's computer.

David stuck his hands into his pockets and said, "What could we possibly be up to?"

"I don't know," Damont said, adjusting his baseball cap. "But it's something."

Wishbone knew it was time for a little action. He edged over to David and whispered, "Psst! Listen. I've thought of a way to stall Damont. With the help of Joe and Sam, I may be able to keep him here for a few minutes. That should give you enough time to deal with Brewster. Got it? . . . No, don't say anything. Okay, here I go."

Wishbone went over to Damont as if he were going to give his ankle a friendly sniff. Instead, he grabbed the lace of one of the skates between his teeth. With a growl, Wishbone jerked back his head, untying the lace.

Damont looked down. "Hey, Talbot, look—your dog's attacking me!"

With the lace still between his teeth, Wishbone managed to say, "David, go!"

David seemed to get the idea. "I'll see you guys later," he said, looking directly at Joe and Sam. "And I do mean later!" David turned and ran toward the dorm building.

"Let go, ya dumb dog!" Damont cried, trying to pull his skate free.

"Fat chance," Wishbone said, keeping his grip. "This jaw of mine is like an iron vise."

"Joe! Sam!" Damont called. "Help me out here!"

Sam turned and saw David charge through the front door of the dorm building. "Sure," she said. "We'll help you out."

Joe smiled at Damont. "Any minute now, we'll start helping you."

After charging up two flights of steps, David stopped in front of Room 316, which he knew was Brewster's dorm room. He knocked at the door, trying to catch his breath.

"Who is it?" Brewster called.

"David Barnes. I need to talk to you about something."

Brewster opened the door, a confused look on his face. "I'm not sure we should be talking today," he said. "Remember, we've got the radio face-off in just a few hours."

"What's the big deal?" David pointed out. "I just need to . . . uh . . . show you something."

"Like what?" Brewster asked.

David stepped into the room, which was littered with clothing, magazines, and empty food containers. Noticing the computer was turned on, David made a move toward it. "I think it'll be easiest if I just show you on the computer. Do you mind?"

Brewster stepped in front of David. "Yeah, I *do* mind. I don't like anyone messing with my computer. What's this about?"

David realized he would have to do a better job as an actor. Immediately. Before Damont came barging into the room. "It's about that silver object I found," David said as naturally as possible. "The one with the symbol on it."

"What about the silver object?" Brewster asked him suspiciously.

David looked Brewster in the eye and said, "It'll be a lot easier if I can just show you on the computer."

Brewster hesitated, then stepped aside. "Okay, but this better be good."

David made his way to the computer. At the keyboard, he typed: 3-8-H-O-A-X.

He waited, watching the screen. Brewster stood behind him, also watching the screen.

Five seconds went by. Nothing happened. Another five seconds went by. Still nothing.

Losing hope, David realized the special phrase should have appeared by then. When David gave the virus a trial run, the phrase had appeared instantly. It was now clear to David that Brewster Kidd was not the on-line alien.

Brewster grabbed David's arm and turned him around. "Hey, what's going on here, Barnes?"

David decided to tell at least part of the truth. "Somebody has been sending anonymous computer messages to me. I wanted to find out who it was, so I sent this person a harmless virus. I thought it might be you, so I needed to check your computer. But I see now that you're innocent. That's it. And I'm . . . uh . . . sorry I bothered you."

The door burst open, and Damont flew into the room, followed by Joe, Sam, and Wishbone. "Watch out for Barnes!" Damont cried, pointing at David. "He's up to something!"

As Brewster, Damont, Joe, and Sam tried to sort things out, David sat at Brewster's desk. He felt an awesome realization crash-landing in his mind.

Yesterday morning, he had set out to prove the on-line alien was a fake. He thought this would be easy. Yet, after using the tools of research, technology, and a little trickery, he had failed to accomplish his goal. That alone didn't prove the alien was real. But it meant David must now consider the possibility that he had been communicating with an extraterrestrial being—a creature from a planet nineteen light-years out in the black depths of the universe.

Chapter Thirteen

David almost had the feeling he was in a spaceship. The control room of the WOAK radio station looked like something from the future—very clean and high-tech. A young guy wearing a leather jacket sat at a console with a large display of controls, meters, and sound decks. This was Kirk, the program engineer.

David took a deep breath, as he tried to stay calm. A digital clock on the wall showed 6:58. The program that aired right before Gilbert's show was finishing up. Gilbert and Brewster stood nearby, and Wishbone waited patiently at David's heels.

"I'll ask you one more time," Gilbert whispered to David. "Does the dog really have to be here?"

"He insisted on following me," David said with a shrug. "It's all right. He never causes any trouble. In fact, I kind of like having him around. He'll be my good-luck charm."

Through a large rectangular window, David could see the broadcast room. A young woman with braided hair sat at a round table and spoke into a microphone. Her upbeat voice came through a speaker in the control room.

"Wasn't that wonderful? I thought you'd like it. But I'm afraid it's time I bid all you fine, friendly folks a good-night. This has been Melissa Sue Ogilvy, bringing you the *Fine and Friendly Folk Hour*. Stay tuned for *Youth Viewpoint*, coming up next."

The engineer inserted a tape into a deck, and a raspy-throated fellow began singing along with a banjo. Gilbert rolled his eyes. David could see he wasn't a big fan of folk music.

"Okay, guys," the engineer said in a laid-back manner. "Take it away."

Melissa entered the control room. Gilbert gave her a wave. Then he led Brewster, David, and Wishbone through the same door into the broadcast room.

Gilbert, Brewster, and David sat around the table in plush swivel chairs. In front of each chair was a microphone with an adjustable stand. Each of the boys put on a headset, which would allow them to hear the program exactly as it was sounding on the air. Wishbone sat on the floor beside David.

Gilbert removed his round eyeglasses and put them in his shirt pocket. He pulled out some notes. Then he picked up a plastic pitcher and poured a glass of water for himself and for each of the other two boys. Finally, he gave Brewster and David the thumbs-up sign. David realized it was almost time to go on the air.

When a digital clock on the wall showed 7:00, the banjo player cross-faded with electronic music. David knew this was Gilbert's theme song. Soon the music stopped, and a sign over the rectangular window lit up with the words "On Air" in bright red.

Gilbert spoke into his microphone, his voice clear and polished. "Good evening. This is *Youth Viewpoint*, and I'm your host, Gilbert Stuart Pickering. Thank you for joining me tonight. I think that we have an interesting program for you."

David felt the butterflies flutter in his stomach. He reached down to give Wishbone a pat on the head to calm himself.

"As I'm sure most of you know by now," Gilbert continued, "this past Friday night, a mysterious green glow was sighted in the skies over Oakdale. Because there is still no explanation for this green glow, I think we are safe in calling it a 'UFO'—an unidentified flying object. This evening we will be discussing the Oakdale UFO, as well as the alien phenomenon in general."

David was especially nervous. He still had not decided what he was or was not going to say about the on-line alien. He took a sip of water from his glass.

"I have two guests with me here in the studio," Gilbert continued. "First, David Barnes, an eighth-grader at Sequoyah Middle School. David was recently the first-place winner in the regional finals of the Young Scientist Competition, and he will soon be moving on to the national finals. Thank you for being here, David."

"Thanks for having me," David spoke into his mike.

"My other guest is Brewster Kidd," Gilbert announced. "Brewster is a sophomore at Oakdale College. He is a UFO enthusiast who operates a Web site devoted to this subject. How are you, Brewster?"

"Great, man," Brewster spoke into his mike. Again, he was wearing the T-shirt announcing "We will find the truth!"

Gilbert folded his hands together. He was very comfortable in his role as on-air radio personality. "The first question that I would like to ask is this: Have E.T.s— or extraterrestrial beings—ever visited the planet Earth? David, what is your opinion?"

David cleared his throat. "There is no conclusive proof that E.T.s have ever visited our planet."

"Brewster," Gilbert said, "same question to you."

Brewster answered without hesitation. "Yes. E.T.s have been visiting our planet for thousands of years."

"Please explain," Gilbert said.

Brewster turned his baseball cap around backward. "There are cave paintings going back to prehistoric times that show flying disks in the sky. And many ancient documents in many different languages refer to strange flying objects. And . . . uh . . . well, who was flying around in those days, if it wasn't aliens?"

"Good question," Gilbert said.

Brewster pressed on. "And, for example, take the pyramids of ancient Egypt. There's no way human beings at that time could have built those things. They're too huge, too perfect, too . . . uh . . . triangular. There are many scholars, myself included, who believe that E.T.s helped the Egyptians build the pyramids."

"I think that Brewster is underestimating human ingenuity," David said. "Sure, a lot of things about ancient civilizations are puzzling. But that doesn't mean alien visitors are the explanation for every single thing we don't understand."

"Let's move up to more recent times," Gilbert suggested. "The past fifty years are often called the 'Flying Saucer Era.' People seem to be seeing them all the time—all over the planet."

"I think there's a good reason for that," David said. "It was about fifty years ago that air travel became widely available. After that, space travel became a reality. The average person was very aware of these changes, and I think these advances fed their imaginations."

"Interesting view," Gilbert said.

"Look," Brewster jumped in, "I don't deny there's a lot of kooks out there. I've met some of them myself. And a lot of these UFO sightings are obviously bunk. But there have been many, many UFO sightings by very reliable people. Policemen, pilots, professors. And what about this thing in Oakdale? Half of the people I know saw it— including both of you guys!"

"Brewster makes a very good point here," Gilbert said. "David, you saw the green glow. What do you believe it was?"

"To be honest," David admitted, "I have no idea."

"Do you think there is any possibility it could have been an alien spacecraft?" Gilbert asked.

David hesitated. "I suppose it's . . . possible."

"But," Gilbert said, "you don't think it's very likely."

David took a sip of water, then spoke. "Well, I didn't say that."

Gilbert raised his eyebrows. "I'm surprised. The other night you seemed almost positive the green glow was *not* an alien spacecraft. Why the change of mind?"

David shifted in his seat. "I don't know that I've changed my mind."

Brewster pointed an accusing finger at David. "You *know* that was an alien spacecraft—don't you? As a matter of fact, you know it better than any of us!" Brewster pounded his hand on the table, causing the microphones to bounce.

Gilbert shot Brewster an annoyed look. "Why do you say that, Brewster?"

Brewster just glared at David. "Let the boy-wonder scientist tell us himself."

David had expected something like this. He knew Brewster would bring up the silver object. When the time came, David figured, he would know how to handle the situation. But now the time was here, and he still wasn't sure what he should or shouldn't say.

"David," Gilbert said, "why would you know better than any of us that the green glow was an alien space-craft? You're not by any chance an alien yourself, are you?"

"Ah, you're on to me," David said with a nervous chuckle.

"Hey," Gilbert said, continuing with the joke, "I've known you all these years without suspecting. Maybe that would explain your high degree of intelligence."

Brewster wasn't laughing, though. He spoke into his mike. "David Barnes has found evidence—real *physical* evidence—that aliens have visited Oakdale."

Gilbert looked puzzled. "David, is this true?"

The words came out before David could stop them. "Well, it might be."

Gilbert leaned forward. "Hmm . . . this is very interesting. Could you explain, please?"

In his mind, very quickly, David once again weighed the pros and cons of telling the truth about the on-line alien. When he came to the cons this time, he found another reason why he should probably keep quiet about the whole thing. If he, David Barnes, winner of the regional finals in the Young Scientist Competition, admitted he might be in contact with an alien creature from outer space, everyone would laugh at him. It was the kind of embarrassment that might take years to live down!

The eyes of both Gilbert and Brewster were focused intensely on David. He saw Kirk watching from the control room. Even Wishbone, David noticed, was gazing up at him. And David knew that everyone he knew, and hundreds of other people, were listening to the program.

He simply didn't know what to say.

Suddenly, Wishbone's head whipped around. David turned to see what had caught the dog's attention. Wishbone was staring at a door on the opposite side from the control room.

The door had a square window in it, and, to David's surprise, the glass cracked right down the middle.

In his headset, David heard Brewster say, "Come on, Barnes, you've stalled on this thing long enough. It's time to speak the truth!"

David turned back to his microphone, puzzled by the cracking glass, which no one else seemed to notice.

Gilbert said, "David, you were about to say that you may have discovered some evidence that an alien craft visited Oakdale."

"Uh . . . well . . ."

Feeling that his mouth was dry as chalk, David reached for his glass of water. Just before he touched it, he pulled back his hand. The glass cracked.

A similar thing happened to Gilbert's glass, then to Brewster's glass. Water leaked out of the broken glasses and flowed like three miniature rivers across the table-top. David and the others stared in total disbelief. But Gilbert began gesturing that David should continue talking anyway.

Seeing movement at the rectangular window, David lifted his head. Kirk was standing up, peering into the broadcast room. Obviously, he, too, had witnessed the mysterious cracking of the glasses.

David's eyes raised to the red "On Air" sign over the window. The glass cover on the sign was cracking. A piece of glass fell to the floor and shattered. With a loud *pop!*, the red light bulb exploded!

It was as if an invisible force was flowing through the room, destroying one thing after another. David

couldn't help but think of the invisible heat ray in *The War of the Worlds*.

David felt frozen in his chair. He was in shock. All he could think was, *It's the alien. It must be. It's real and it's here. Maybe it's just reminding me to tell people that it is among us. Or maybe . . . maybe . . . maybe the war has begun!*

It was time for David to reveal everything he knew.

He leaned toward his microphone. "Here's what I have to say. This may sound very strange, but—"

Kirk's voice was heard over a loudspeaker in the room. "Gilbert, something crazy is going on out there. I need to check it out. Announce that we'll be going to music for five minutes."

Sounding less controlled than usual, Gilbert spoke into his mike. "We are experiencing some technical difficulty in the studio. While we sort this out, we're going to play some music for you. But please stay tuned. We'll be back in just five minutes."

David heard a song in his headset. It was the same raspy-voiced folk singer who had played at the end of the earlier program.

David took off his headset and looked around the studio. Everyone's reaction was different. The engineer was darting around the control room, quickly checking over the equipment. Brewster was dipping a finger into the spilled water, his mouth wide open with wonder. Wishbone was scampering back and forth, his ears standing straight up.

Gilbert removed his headset and said in a hushed voice, "What in the world is happening?"

David didn't know how to answer that. He had absolutely no idea what just happened, or what the next few seconds would bring.

Chapter Fourteen

For the past two minutes, a high-pitched sound had been screaming in Wishbone's ears.

"Stop it!" Wishbone barked, as he ran around the broadcast room. "This is like sitting in the front row at a rock concert. And I'm talking heavy metal!"

Suddenly the sound stopped.

Wishbone twitched his ears a few times to clear them out. He paused to look around the room. The others in the room had noticed the breaking glass, but not the sound. It was too high-pitched for them to hear.

Brewster, after removing his headset, rose slowly to his feet and said in an excited voice, "They are here! This is the moment I've been waiting for my whole life! The government can deny that aliens crash-landed near Roswell, New Mexico! But the government can't deny *this!* The aliens are here in my hometown! And I'm going to make sure the world knows it!"

Everyone ignored Brewster.

Gilbert put his glasses back on and looked around the room. Then he went to the control room and opened the door. "Find anything yet?" he asked Kirk.

"No," the engineer said. "I was worried some of the sound equipment may have been causing the problem, but so far everything checks out fine. Nothing else is breaking, is it?"

"No," Gilbert replied. "It seems to have stopped."

Wishbone went to David, who was deep in thought. "David, listen to me. I think Brewster is right. I think that *was* the alien causing all that stuff to happen. When we go back on the air, we need to report what's going on. Both of us!"

David was so lost in thought, he didn't seem to hear.

Brewster began pacing around the table. "We need to get the word out! And we need to do it before the government tries to stop us! Is anybody listening to me?" In his excitement, Brewster tripped over Wishbone.

"Hey, watch it!" Wishbone snapped.

Gilbert tapped Brewster on the shoulder. "Brewster, I hear someone running down the hallway. Maybe it's the marines."

Panic spread across Brewster's face. "Really? Are you serious?"

"Actually, I'm not," Gilbert said with a grin.

"This is not a joke," Brewster said, pointing an angry finger at Gilbert. "The military might very well be here soon. I'll bet they've been monitoring the town ever since that green thing showed up around here. We need to get the word out."

"For once, Brewster speaks the truth," Wishbone told David. "The public has to be warned. We are in the middle of a national crisis. I wonder if the President is listening to this program."

Suddenly David stood. "Gilbert, I'm going to the water fountain. I'm thirsty, and all the glasses here are broken."

"Okay, but hurry back," Gilbert said.

"Come on," David said, waving to Wishbone, "I'll bet you could use some water, too."

"That might be a good idea," Wishbone said. "I should freshen my throat before I make my first radio appearance."

David opened the door that had the cracked window, and Wishbone followed him into a hallway. David passed a water fountain and kept on walking.

"Hey, David," Wishbone called. "You missed the water . . ."

David continued down the hall, soon stopping to examine a window. Wishbone noticed that this window was also cracked. "Yes," David said, as he touched the windowpane, "the sound could have been coming from outside."

David walked farther down the hall, soon opening a door that led outside. "David," Wishbone called, "it's not time to head for the hills yet. First we have a citizen's duty to warn the public about the alien invasion!"

David stepped outside, and Wishbone followed. The last light of dusk hung in the air, giving the evening a weird sense of motion. The trees and shrubs seemed to wave, and the nearby buildings looked as if they might be moving around a bit. As far as Wishbone could tell, however, there was no one around.

David knelt down to Wishbone, a determined look in his eyes. "Is there any way you can find where that sound was coming from? I suspect that a high-frequency sound cracked the glass—a sound not heard by humans, but heard by dogs."

"I *know* where it was coming from," Wishbone replied. "The mind of an alien!"

"That's why you turned your head toward the sound

114

a few seconds before anything actually cracked. Right, Wishbone? Now, I need to know exactly where the sound was coming from. It couldn't have been too far from here," David said.

Wishbone gave his side a scratch. "Yeah, but even if the alien is nearby, it could be invisible. I don't smell Wanda around, so I'm pretty sure it slipped out of her body. It probably got tired of wearing all those weird clothes."

David rubbed his face with frustration. "How can I make you understand me?"

"I understand you fine, David. But even if I *could* find this alien, I'm not real eager to meet it face to face—if it even *has* a face!"

David seemed to focus all his energy on the dog. "Please, Wishbone. Please find where that sound is coming from!"

"Okay," Wishbone said reluctantly. "But you owe me big-time. And I'm talking a year's supply of sirloin steaks. If we survive, that is."

Wishbone's sense of hearing was so sophisticated, he could almost draw a map in his mind of traveling sound waves—even tracking sounds he hadn't heard for several minutes.

Wishbone raised his ears, calling on all his powers of sound memory. He began to hear, or almost hear, the high-pitched screech that had invaded the studio. Slowly, Wishbone tried to find the path the sound waves might have taken. He walked alongside the WOAK building, then turned toward the street. Then he angled toward the wooden WOAK sign that stood on the lawn.

Wishbone's heart was racing with anticipation. He was heading straight into the unknown—armed with nothing but his wits and his teeth. And that might not be enough.

Up ahead a shadow began to form into a mysterious shape. Through the eerie twilight, Wishbone saw Wanda Gilmore walking toward him. Her eyes were blank, her steps heavy and robotic. Facing Wishbone, Wanda lifted her hands and peeled off her face as if it were a Halloween mask. She now had a head resembling that of a gigantic green grasshopper!

Wishbone blinked. Wanda was gone. He realized it was all in his imagination.

Get a grip, Wishbone thought. *Things are scary enough without making them even worse!*

Wishbone stopped near the WOAK sign, which was surrounded by low shrubbery. "It was coming from right there," he whispered to David. "Just inside those leafy things. I'll take a look. But if I don't come back, well . . . make sure Joe knows I was a hero up until the bitter end."

Wishbone stuck his muzzle inside the shrubbery.

There it stood—the alien!

It looked like no living thing that Wishbone had ever seen.

Wait a second, Wishbone thought. *That's not an alien. It's . . .*

David knelt down and pulled back some of the shrubbery. He and Wishbone both saw a boxlike object, a cylindrical item, and an electrical device.

"A speaker, a battery, and an amplifier!" David said with excitement. "The hoaxer strikes again. I *knew* it. He or she wanted me to think that the alien was causing the glass to crack. But it was just this sound equipment. I guess our practical joker is long gone by now. Wishbone, you're a real hero, boy. Come on!"

As Wishbone hurried after David on their way back toward the WOAK building, he realized David was right. Someone had used the battery-powered amplifier and speaker to project high-frequency sound waves that caused the glass in the studio to crack. It was one of those scientific phenomena. Obviously, the culprit was the same person who had sent the on-line messages and left the silver object in David's yard.

Wishbone realized something else. If he thought a high-frequency sound was an alien, he might also believe a low-frequency sound was an alien. Which meant the low humming sound that he heard earlier might also be coming from some electrical device.

But then, Wishbone wondered, *why has Wanda been acting so strange?*

As soon as David and Wishbone entered the broadcast room, Gilbert called, "Get back in your seat. Kirk couldn't find any problem, so we're continuing with the show."

David sat in his chair and put on his headset. After Wishbone pawed David's legs several times, David lifted the dog into an empty chair. Wishbone examined the microphone in front of him. It was way too high. He put his front paws on the table and managed to lower the microphone with his muzzle. "Okay," Wishbone told the others, "I'm all set."

The engineer pointed at Gilbert, and Gilbert spoke into his mike. "Once again, this is *Youth Viewpoint*, back on the air. We are about to hear some really amazing news. David, you were about to say you found evidence that aliens have visited Oakdale. Could you explain this, please?"

Brewster's eyes seemed to burn a hole into David.

"Yes, I can," David said with confidence. "But what I was about to explain is this. Someone has been trying to make me *think* an alien has visited Oakdale. But it's obviously a prank, and nothing we need to take seriously."

Brewster pounded the table, once more causing the microphones to bounce. "Why are you backing down all of a sudden? Did someone get to you on the way to the water fountain? I wouldn't doubt it! The government is everywhere!"

David smiled. "I assure you the government didn't get to me on the way to the water fountain. Nor did anyone else. Now, let's return the discussion to the high level we started at. You know, I was recently talking with a professor at Oakdale College about a concept known as the 'Goldilocks Zone.'"

Gilbert seemed disappointed, and Brewster looked so mad that there might have been smoke coming out of his ears. But Wishbone understood David's reasoning. David didn't want to give satisfaction to the hoaxer by going into detail about the hoaxes. Wishbone respected his decision and kept quiet.

David dominated the rest of the program, speaking in a very knowledgeable way about the possibility of aliens ever visiting the planet Earth. He mentioned the impossibility of anything traveling faster than the speed of light. But, based on his conversation with Dr. Isaacs, he also discussed how intelligent extraterrestrials might be living a lot closer to Earth than previously realized.

All the while, Brewster tried to claim the technical problems were caused by an alien. But without David to back him up, the theory didn't come across as very believable. Nor could he get David to talk about the silver object. At one point, Brewster muttered in disgust, "This is just like Roswell."

When the digital clock showed 7:29, Gilbert said, "It seems we are out of time. I thank you for joining me. I'm your host, Gilbert Stuart Pickering, and this has been *Youth Viewpoint.* Stay tuned for WOAK's next program, *A Thousand and One Tips for Raising Your Kids and Tending Your Plants.*" Gilbert rolled his eyes.

The engineer inserted a tape, which played Gilbert's electronic theme music. But Wishbone wasn't quite ready for the program to end. There was still something that needed to be said.

Wishbone cleared his throat and leaned toward the microphone. "Ladies and gentlemen, fellow animals . . . and anyone else out there who might be listening, this is the voice of Wishbone. Yes, that very handsome Jack Russell terrier many of you have had the pleasure to meet."

Wishbone wondered if his voice was coming out too squeaky. He lowered it to a more dignified tone.

"I just want to clear up something that may have been misunderstood. There is no threat of an alien invasion in Oakdale. I repeat—there is no threat of an alien invasion of Oakdale."

119

Wishbone enjoyed the fact that his voice was now being broadcast to homes all over town. Maybe all over the country. Maybe all over the universe!

"Everyone, please stay calm. It is of the greatest importance that we all stay calm. The crisis is over."

Chapter Fifteen

Despite all the recent excitement, Oakdale looked as calm as ever to David. He was walking home with Wishbone and Gilbert. It was dark now, and porch lights glowed on a block lined with attractive homes. David figured the people there, like most everyone else in town, were enjoying a quiet Sunday night.

And yet, somewhere in this peaceful town, David thought, *there lurks a hoaxer.*

Gilbert chuckled. "Well, to date, that was probably my most bizarre program. Brewster ranting and raving about an alien, a dog in the studio, unidentifiable technical difficulties . . ."

"Actually," David said, "the whole thing was more bizarre than you realize."

"What do you mean?" Gilbert asked.

David decided to confide in Gilbert. He told him about the on-line alien and how, with Wishbone's assistance, he had discovered the cause of the mysterious cracking glass.

"I see," Gilbert said when the story was done. "So what happened with the glass was just part of a prank. I guess it was done to push you toward talking about the on-line alien on the air. Not a bad plan, even though it didn't quite work. Hmm . . . I wonder who this prankster might be."

"I don't know," David said. "But I'd sure like to find out."

"Maybe it was someone jealous of your success in the Young Scientist Competition," Gilbert suggested. "Another one of the contestants. The prankster must be a person with some basic knowledge of science, not to mention computers."

"You don't think Toby could have done this, do you? He fits the bill. And I know he was real disappointed his project didn't make it to the regionals."

"Toby? I doubt it. There's not a mean bone in his body."

"I guess you're right," David said.

Soon the two boys and dog stopped in front of Gilbert's house. "We should continue this conversation later," Gilbert said. "I'd like to help you to unmask this master of deception. You know me. I'm always eager for a big challenge."

Gilbert extended his hand, and David shook it.

But something Gilbert said was buzzing in David's ears. *I'm always eager for a big challenge.* Gilbert had said something similar two nights ago. Just that morning, David had suspected Gilbert as the on-line alien. However, he had ruled Gilbert out, figuring if Gilbert wanted to pull an Orson Welles–style hoax on his radio show, there would be much easier ways than to do it through David. But, then again, *Gilbert liked a big challenge.*

Gilbert was walking toward his front porch. "Hey," David called out, causing Gilbert to turn. "I finished *The War of the Worlds* last night. You were right. H. G. Wells is fantastic. Do you have any other books by him that I could borrow?"

"Sure," Gilbert replied. "I've got several of his books. Come on in. I'll lend them to you."

David and Wishbone followed Gilbert into the house. The boys spent a few minutes talking with Gilbert's parents, then went to Gilbert's room. Gilbert had nice stuff—elaborate models of military aircraft, expensive stereo equipment, a giant lava lamp, and a sleek new computer.

David wondered if this computer could be where the on-line alien came from. It was certainly worth a test.

"Wow! Nice machine," David said, going to the computer. "This is a brand-new model, isn't it? And it's got that new type of processor."

"Yes. My parents gave it to me for my birthday. It's ultra-fast."

"Do you mind if I check it out?"

"Uh . . . no. I guess not."

David tapped the start-up key. As the computer came to life, Gilbert began to search his shelves for his H. G. Wells books. David felt a sense of anticipation as he watched the icons jump onto the screen. He noticed Wishbone was also watching.

David realized there was a problem with the Gilbert scenario. Gilbert had been sitting next to David in the studio when the glass-cracking took place. But David figured Gilbert was smart enough to get around that somehow. Then David remembered something interesting—Gilbert had put his glasses in his pocket when the radio program began.

The computer finished booting up. David flexed his fingers. At the keyboard, he typed: "3-8-H-O-A-X."

He held his breath. One, two, three seconds went by.

Bright red letters jumped on the screen. They spelled: "I am watching YOU!"

David heard a book tumble to the floor. He and Wishbone both turned toward Gilbert, who was looking at the screen.

"That's funny," Gilbert said, stooping to pick up the fallen book. "I wonder where that came from."

A surge of excitement was flowing through David's body. It was similar to the feeling he got when he had finally solved a difficult scientific or technical problem. But David forced himself to remain cool and composed so his words would have more effect. "The message came from me," David said. "You're the on-line alien, Gilbert. And I caught you with a virus. Kind of like what happens in *The War of the Worlds*, isn't it?"

A long moment passed in silence. Slowly, a smile inched its way across Gilbert's face. "Excellent, Barnes. You discovered the truth about the alien, and you did it in a most brilliant way. Congratulations." Suddenly the smile faded. "Hey, that virus won't cause any harm to my computer, will it?"

"No. It won't cause a bit of harm to your brand-new, ultra-fast computer."

"Oh, good," Gilbert said with relief.

David wasn't sure how angry he ought to be. On the one hand, Gilbert had involved him in an interesting battle of wits between two top scientific minds. But, on the other hand, Gilbert had played a mean trick on him. A trick that could have embarrassed David in front of everyone.

David asked, "Why did you do it, Gilbert?"

Gilbert sat in a chair and straightened his glasses. He didn't seem upset that David had caught him red-handed. Nor did he show any guilt for what he had done.

"It was just one of those crazy things," Gilbert said with a shrug. "I mean, when I asked you to be on my show, I had no plans of pulling this prank. I just thought you would be a good guest. It came to me later, when we were walking home from Pepper Pete's. Somehow we got talking about *The War of the Worlds*."

David sat at the desk, and Wishbone took a seat on the floor beside him. "And that made you think of the 1938 radio dramatization of the story," David guessed. "The one that caused a national panic."

"I didn't even know you knew about that. But, yes, that's right. I thought it might be fun to do something similar on my show. Not a national panic, but . . . you know . . . some kind of hoax. And I already had the green UFO to help me."

"But the hoax had to present a real challenge."

Gilbert gave a nod. "Yes. For me, that was the main attraction. Immediately, I thought of your argument with Brewster in Pepper Pete's. You were going on about how it was impossible for aliens to visit our planet. I figured if I could make you, David Barnes, believe there was an alien in Oakdale, and admit it on the show, well, that would be quite an accomplishment."

David felt his face flush with heat. Now he was getting angry. "So this whole thing was done just so you could have a little bit of entertainment? At my expense?"

"Look, I never meant any harm," Gilbert said. "It was just meant as a friendly battle of wits."

David spoke sharply. "Well, I don't feel very friendly right now. I feel like the subject of a science experiment!"

Gilbert glanced at the computer screen, which still announced: "I am watching YOU!" Then he looked at the floor. He was at a loss for words.

Suddenly, David realized there might be another

reason for Gilbert's actions. Gilbert Stuart Pickering liked to be the best at everything. He wore nice clothes, made almost perfect grades, and maybe it was why he had his own radio program. But David had beat him at something—the Young Scientist Competition.

"I'm working on a theory," David told Gilbert. "I think you were upset that I, not you, made it to the national finals of the Young Scientist Competition. And maybe, deep down, that had something to do with why you pulled this prank on me. You lost the challenge of creating a winning science project, so you figured out a way to get the best of someone who did."

Gilbert met David's gaze. "Maybe so," he confessed. "I mean, your cloud-making project was terrific. Really. You figured out how to create genuine cumulus clouds without the use of a coolant. That was awesome. But so was my project. I don't know. Maybe I felt the judges favored you because a project on the greenhouse effect was so . . . politically correct."

David could see that Gilbert was indeed upset about losing the competition. But now that David understood the truth about Gilbert's motivation, he found the prank a little more acceptable. Or at least understandable. Now the detective in David was curious to know some of the details of how Gilbert pulled off the hoax.

"I don't like this hoax business one little bit," Wishbone told Gilbert with a growl in his voice. "From now on, pal, you'd better watch yourself. David and I don't like to be messed around with."

David gave Wishbone's back a scratch. "I know you're good with computers," David told Gilbert, "so I understand how you pulled off all the on-line trickery. But what was that silver thing?"

Gilbert's eyes took on a devious glint. "When we were in Pepper Pete's, do you remember I said my uncle was an aeronautical engineer?"

"Uh-huh," Wishbone said.

"Yes, I do," David replied. "You said he does cutting-edge research."

"I got that thing from him. It's a fragment from a new type of material he created. It's designed to be light-weight, yet able to withstand extremely high temperatures. Supposedly, planes in the near future will be made from something like this. The material is very new. That's why no one at the college was able to identify it. The little symbol . . . well . . . I just engraved that myself."

David gave the desk a tap. "I should have remembered what you said about your uncle."

"Don't feel bad," Wishbone told David. "I missed that connection myself."

"You also should have realized," Gilbert said, "that I knew a lot about high-frequency sounds because of my science project—"

David finished the thought. "Which was about how dolphins locate objects underwater through the use of sound waves. Of course!"

Wishbone scratched the carpet with his paw. "Yes, of course! Of course!"

"I got to be sort of an expert on the subject," Gilbert explained. "That's how I was able to get the distance and high-frequency tone just right for those special effects in the studio. I didn't want too many things to break. And I didn't want the control room damaged. There's very expensive equipment there. I also put my glasses safely away. And, in case you're wondering,

I operated the amplifier with a remote control." Gilbert reached into his pocket and pulled out a small rectangular device.

"Ah, yes!" Wishbone cried out. "You see, everything is remote control these days!"

"Pretty impressive, huh?" Gilbert boasted.

"So impressive," David said evenly, "maybe the manager of the radio station should know about it."

Gilbert stuffed the remote control back in his pocket. "Uh . . . no . . . don't do that. If he found out I was responsible for this, he'd probably cancel me."

"Aha!" Wishbone cried out. "Now the shoe's on the other paw! Isn't it?"

"You should have thought of that before," David said.

"Well, I didn't think I'd be *caught!*" exclaimed Gilbert. "I mean, how was I supposed to know you'd bring a dog into the studio?"

Wishbone stood up, offended. "And what's wrong with that? If you ask me, there ought to be a few dog shows on the air. Hey, that gives me an . . ." Wishbone sat back down so he could pursue his new idea.

David stroked his chin, as if thinking about something. "Maybe I won't tell the manager. Maybe I'll just get even by playing some prank on *you.*"

"What sort of prank?" Gilbert asked.

"I don't know yet. Besides, I wouldn't tell you, anyway. But it'll be something that catches you off guard when you least expect it. Maybe next week, maybe ten years from now. And I'll be sure to arrange it so you make a total fool of yourself in front of lots of people. The way I almost did."

Gilbert pushed back some blond hair that had fallen out of place. "Uh . . . David, I'd rather you didn't do that.

Look, I'll tell the station manager about the hoax myself. And I'll pay for all the damaged glass."

"I don't know," David said. "This might be fun. *A real challenge*, if you know what I mean."

Gilbert stood up, showing a hint of desperation. "How about this? Next week on my show, I'll make a public confession of the hoax. People won't like it, but then they might respect me for being honest. Hopefully, the station manager will, too. And I'll make a public promise not to do anything like this again."

"I think that's a good idea," David replied.

Wishbone knew that David's threat to get even wasn't serious. He just wanted to give Gilbert a taste of his own medicine. Wishbone walked over to Gilbert and nudged one of the boy's legs. "You know, speaking about radio shows—"

"Then you'll drop the idea about getting back at me?" Gilbert asked David. "Come on. Otherwise, I'll never know if I can ever trust you about anything."

David stood to face Gilbert. "That's the problem with mean pranks. Afterward, people have trouble trusting the person who masterminded them."

Gilbert took a moment to consider that. It seemed to be sinking in that his actions were as inconsiderate as they were clever. "You're right," he said, seeming to mean it. "I'm sorry, David. I really hope this thing hasn't destroyed our friendship."

"Apology accepted," David said. He offered his hand, and Gilbert gave it a firm shake.

Wishbone nudged Gilbert's leg again. "I'll tell you what. David and I will go easy on you—but only on one condition."

Gilbert knelt down to pet Wishbone. "Hi, there, fella. From what I hear, you're one intelligent dog."

"Thank you," Wishbone replied. "Now, here's the deal. You talk to the station manager and tell him you have a suggestion for a new radio show. It'll be called *The World According to Wishbone*. I'll be the host, of course. Every program will feature fascinating guests and discussions on a wide range of topics. Current events, fashion, cat-chasing, tips on burying bones. The possibilities are endless."

Gilbert smiled. "Hey, look at this dog. I think he's trying to tell me something."

"Yes, I'm trying to tell you something!" Wishbone practically shouted. "I'm telling you that I was born to be a star!"

Chapter Sixteen

The stars glimmered in a deep black sky. As David sat on the steps of the Talbots' front porch, he picked out a few of his favorite constellations. Wishbone lay beside him, while Joe and Sam sat on the swing chair.

When David and Wishbone got home, they found everyone waiting at the Barneses' house, where they had all listened to the radio program. David told all of them the whole story about the on-line alien, from its first appearance to its final capture. Soon after that, the kids went outside. It had been a long day, but now that everything was resolved, David felt a sense of satisfaction.

"I have a confession to make," Sam said, as she and Joe swung back and forth in the swing chair. "I'm a little disappointed that it didn't turn out to be a real alien."

"So am I," Joe offered.

"Me, too," David agreed.

"You?" Joe said with surprise. "But, David, you spent so much time trying to prove it *wasn't* a real alien."

David showed a slight smile. "Why do you think a scientist tries to prove something isn't true? Because he's interested in finding out if it *might be*."

"Of course," Sam remarked, "now we don't have to worry about being disintegrated by an invisible heat ray. Or something along those lines."

"That's the scary thing about aliens," Joe put in. "If and when we finally meet up with them, there's no telling how dangerous they might be. Then, again, they might turn out to be the nicest guys in the universe."

David continued to examine the stars. They seemed to have a faint twinkle, but David knew that was just an optical illusion.

"H. G. Wells summed it up perfectly toward the end of *The War of the Worlds*," David told his friends. "He wrote: 'We can never anticipate the unseen good or evil that may come upon us suddenly from out of space.'"

Both Joe and Sam looked up at the sky.

David reached over to ruffle the fur on Wishbone's back. "All my life," he said, "I've wanted to understand as much as I can about the physical world. These past few days, I've realized one of the reasons why. There is nothing—and I really mean *nothing*—so frightening as the unknown.

And what's more unknown to us than extraterrestrial life?"

"Speaking of unknown," Joe said, "we still don't know what that green glow was."

"And I think it might have had some kind of power to it," Sam mentioned.

"Why do you say that?" David asked.

Sam stopped the swing chair from moving. "This man on my block, Mr. Anderson, works for the electric company. He says his office has been getting a lot of calls this weekend. Electrical meters all over town are going screwy. They're not working right, and they're giving off a very low humming sound that can only be detected with special equipment. Mr. Anderson thinks the green glow may have somehow caused the problem."

Joe jumped off the swing chair. "See, I told you there were aliens in that thing!"

As much as David wanted to agree with Joe on this matter, he was still too much of a scientist to jump to conclusions. "Well, even if the green glow was a natural phenomenon," he said reasonably, "it could have given off an electrical force that interfered with the meters."

"David is absolutely right," Wishbone pointed out. "You see, electromagnetism is a very interesting force. It's . . . Oh, what's the use? When it comes to science, no one listens to the dog. Hey, wait! . . . Electrical meter . . . low humming . . . Guys, I'll be right back!"

Wishbone leaped off the porch and ran toward Wanda's house. Around the side of the house he found a gray-metal box with a dial on it. Wishbone knew this was the electric meter. When Wishbone stood right next to the meter, he realized the low humming sound was at its loudest. But the sound was still so low, not even Wishbone had been able to locate exactly where it was coming from.

What do you know! Wishbone thought. *Yet another mystery solved. Boy, when it comes to detective work, I am the top dog!*

A voice pierced the night. "Wishbone, you're not bothering my flowers, are you?"

Wishbone turned to see Wanda, who had just come out of the Barneses' house. She had a green scarf draped around her neck, and she wore purple-polka-dot pants. Strange as she looked, Wishbone was glad to know it was just regular ol' Wanda.

Wishbone and Wanda both walked toward the Talbots' house. When they met by the Talbots' porch, Wishbone told Wanda, "No, I'm not bothering your flowers. And, by the way, your electric meter is on the blink."

Wanda stretched her arms and tilted her head upward. "Ah, look at that sky! Isn't it a gorgeous night?"

Joe said, "You're in a good mood, Miss Gilmore."

"Yes, I am, Joe," Wanda said enthusiastically. "And I'll tell you why. Remember the other night when I ran out of my house to look at the green glow? I was wearing my fuzzy slippers and I slipped. I must have pulled something in my back. For the past two days it's really been bothering me."

"Oh, I'm sorry to hear that," Sam said with concern.

Wanda placed a hand on her back. "I tried everything to fix it. First I put an electrical back massager in a chair, but that didn't help much. Then I tried meditating while standing in a yoga position, but that didn't help. Then I tried scented incense, healing crystals, and eating tofu, which is a very nutritious health food. Still no relief.

But, a few minutes ago, suddenly my back felt as good as new! So that's why I'm in a great mood. Well, I'd better dash on home. I need to bake a cake for the historical society's luncheon tomorrow."

"Maybe you'd better not dash," Joe suggested. "You don't want to hurt your back again."

Wanda gave a nod, then *walked* to her house.

Well, I guess that's another mystery solved, Wishbone thought. *All that stuff Wanda mentioned fits with what I saw going on at her house. I shouldn't have been fooled so easily, but, well, okay, I jumped to conclusions. It happens to the best of us.*

Wishbone sat beside David on the porch step. He still heard the low humming sound, but now that he knew what it was, it didn't bother him the least little bit.

Joe and Sam resumed swinging in the swing chair. "Look at all those stars," Sam said quietly. "After this weekend, I don't know if I'll ever see them again in quite the same way."

Wishbone spoke up. "Hey, does anybody know what the brightest star in our sky is? Sirius. Also known as the Dog Star."

"I wonder how many stars are there," Joe said. "In the whole universe."

"No one knows," David replied. "Probably zillions."

"And how many of those stars do you think have planets around them?" Sam asked.

"Could be a billion," David answered. "Which means there might be trillions of planets."

"Do you think Earth is the only planet that has intelligent life?" Joe asked.

"It could be," David said. "But it doesn't seem very likely. Hey, if there is any intelligent life out there, maybe Wishbone will figure out a way to contact them. He already found one alien for me." David gave Wishbone's back an affectionate pat.

Wishbone looked up at David. "I'll do my very best. From this distance, I can't smell or see or hear them. But I'm a dog, remember. I've got all sorts of senses you guys don't even know about. And I would love to make contact with creatures from another planet. It would be a giant leap for all Mankind. Not to mention Dogkind!"

Then Wishbone raised his eyes to the sky. He noticed Sirius, the Dog Star, was shining even brighter than usual.

About Alexander Steele

Alexander Steele writes books, plays, and screenplays for both children and adults. *Case of the On-Line Alien* is his second book for the WISHBONE Mysteries series, his first being *Tale of the Missing Mascot*. He has also written *Moby Dog* for The Adventures of Wishbone series.

Mystery and history are Alexander's favorite subjects. He has written nine detective novels for young readers, and is currently working on a novel for adults that examines the origins of detectives—in both fiction and real life. Among Alexander's plays is the award-winning *One Glorious Afternoon*, which focuses on William Shakespeare and his fellow actors at the Globe Theatre in London, England.

Alexander was first introduced to *The War of the Worlds* when he saw the super-cool movie version of the book. Later, he read some books by H. G. Wells and, like David Barnes, spent many late nights turning their pages. He gradually realized that these stories were not only great science fiction tales, but also interesting comments on society. Indeed, Wells also wrote philosophy books and a book about the history of the world! Alexander would like to think that Mr. Wells would be both frightened and pleased by *Case of the On-Line Alien*.

Alexander lives in New York City, where he has sighted a few people he believes might be of extraterrestrial origin.